The Broken Duke

(THE 1797 CLUB BOOK 3)

By

USA Today Bestseller
Jess Michaels

THE BROKEN DUKE

The 1797 Club Book 3

www.1797Club.com

Copyright © Jesse Petersen, 2017

ISBN-13: 978-1947770003
ISBN-10: 1947770004

For more information, contact Jess Michaels
www.AuthorJessMichaels.com

To contact the author:
Email: Jess@AuthorJessMichaels.com
Twitter www.twitter.com/JessMichaelsbks
Facebook: www.facebook.com/JessMichaelsBks

Jess Michaels raffles a gift certificate EVERY month to members of her newsletter, so sign up on her website: http://www.authorjessmichaels.com/

DEDICATION

Graham was one of my favorite heroes I've ever written. My hope is that you'll fall in love with him as deeply as Adelaide does.

Thank you for all your support and love for the 1797 Club series.

This book, as all my books, is for Michael. I don't shine if you don't shine. Thanks for always letting me put my back on you.

CHAPTER ONE

October 1810

Graham Everly, Duke of Northfield, sat in the corner of a dingy tavern, a mug of ale souring in his fist. He'd been drinking, but he wasn't drunk. Yet. He wanted to remedy that fact as quickly as possible.

But before he could take another sip, two men moved through the crowd and steered toward him. Ewan Hoffstead, Duke of Donburrow, and his cousin Matthew Cornwallis, Duke of Tyndale, both carried their own drinks, and they exchanged a not-so-subtle look before they retook their seats at his table. Graham sighed, for he was hoping the two had left already. It seemed they had not.

But then, neither of them had left his side very often in the past two months. He'd tried to avoid them, as he'd been avoiding all his friends since "the incident," as he liked to call it. But Ewan and Tyndale were relentless.

As if to demonstrate that point, Ewan dug into his overcoat pocket and drew out a small notebook and stubby charcoal pencil. He scribbled for a moment as Graham watched him. Ewan had been mute since birth, and writing was his main form of communication to friends and family.

He pushed the notebook over and Graham read the neat, even line of words written there. *"Don't sit here all night. Don't drink yourself stupid."*

Graham shoved the notebook back and glared at him. "Thanks, mate. You know, it's possible drinking won't make me stupid. I may just be stupid without the help."

Ewan shook his head with a flash of a grin at the self-deprecation, but there was no mistaking the concern in his dark eyes.

Tyndale seemed no less worried as he leaned in and said, "Come on, you can't deny it even if you make light of it. You've been stalking London pubs for two months, avoiding everyone who loves you. I recognize the signs, you know."

Graham flinched. If anyone would, Tyndale did. After all, the woman he'd loved had died years ago, devastating Tyndale down to his core. A fact which made Graham's problems seem very small. But he really didn't want to discuss this topic. It was exactly why he'd been avoiding his entire group of friends all this time. He didn't want to commiserate. He wanted to forget.

"I'm with you two, aren't I?" he growled, once again making light of the subject he could see the other two were determined to address.

Ewan wrote something and shoved it over. *"Well, we don't love you."*

Despite himself, Graham began to laugh and Matthew joined in. For a moment, his troubles faded, but then they settled back on his shoulders. And this time it didn't seem like he could avoid the topic as easily as he had been able to before.

"Look," he said, pushing his drink aside. "I know I should get over this. But Crestwood was one of my best friends and he betrayed me with what happened with Margaret."

Matthew's expression softened. "She was your fiancée, Northfield. And it's a complicated situation given their feelings for each other, but no matter the circumstances, Simon shouldn't have...*taken* her like he did. It *was* wrong."

"No one begrudges you the pain you must feel," Ewan added. "We only worry about how you choose to express it."

Graham stared at the words on Ewan's notebook and sighed. He had been engaged to Margaret Rylon, the sister of another of their group, for seven long years. He hadn't ever loved her, even though he'd tried desperately to make that feeling come into his heart.

But the idea that Simon would betray him...Simon, who had been like his brother since they were thirteen...well, that kept him up at night. "It isn't about her, you know."

Matthew nodded and there was that flicker of sadness in his expression again. "I know."

"We need to get you back into the world. It's time, don't you think?" Ewan wrote, then clapped Graham on the shoulder.

Graham shifted. They were right, of course. He'd been hiding long enough, sulking and stewing as the rest of the world went on without him. At some point, he had to get himself together. He had to face Society and the friends he had been avoiding and the future that now seemed wide open and utterly different than it had been in the years he was resigned to a loveless arranged marriage.

"What do you have in mind?" he asked, slow and uncertain.

Ewan and Matthew exchanged a grin before Ewan scribbled, "There's a play tonight that you must see. Everyone is talking about it. Come out with us."

Graham let out a long sigh. "I don't know. The theatre? That's a big leap from hiding out in pubs."

"We'll sneak in late," Tyndale assured him. "No one will have to know you're there unless you want them to. Come on. It's better than passing out behind some tavern and making Ewan and me carry you home, isn't it?"

Graham shot Ewan a look. He was a massive man, well over six feet and built out of pure muscle. "You've never carried anything home in your life, Tyndale, not if your cousin is with you."

As Ewan grinned, Matthew elbowed him and shot Graham a look. "Does that mean you'll go, bad company as you are?"

Graham nodded. "Yes. I'll do it." He sighed again. "At least it will distract me."

The other two men looked happy at his decision as they all

rose to leave the tavern, but Graham didn't feel the same. The last thing he wanted was to drag himself off to a public event where everyone could judge him. Not to mention waste a few hours watching some play that would probably be terrible.

But after all they'd done to support him, he owed it to his friends to try. And it was, after all, only one night.

Graham sat in a box overlooking the dark stage. Though he, Ewan and Tyndale had come into the theatre just before the rise of the curtain, it had not diminished the interest in his being there. Even now he felt the eyes of the crowd below on him, he'd heard the whispers of his name when he took his seat.

His cheeks and chest burned with humiliation and renewed anger. Thanks to Simon, his *friend*, the world pitied and judged and talked about him. He'd spent a lifetime trying to avoid anything that would make others do those very things and here he was. Exactly where he didn't want to be, and he glanced at the exit behind him.

"Don't run," Ewan wrote, nudging him with an elbow to force him to read it in the dim light.

Graham folded his arms. Apparently he was becoming predictable. "I'm not going anywhere," he grunted as the lights on the stage rose and the curtain along with it.

He settled back to watch what would surely be a terrible performance, as many of these plays were. The theatre was more a place for those who wished to be seen, rather than for anything worth watching. But to his surprise, the usual din of noise of people chatting faded and everyone seemed to truly pay attention as a woman entered the stage.

He leaned forward as she began to speak. She was beautiful, with honey blonde hair that fell around her shoulders in waves. She had a fine, clear voice that carried even to the rafters. But what stood out most was her confidence. As she strode across the stage, it was impossible not to watch her every move.

"I pray for death," she said, her voice trembling with what felt like true emotion. "To free me from this pain. Strike me down, won't you? End this farce of a life."

Graham stared. She was *good*.

He watched for a while, enthralled as another actor came on stage and the woman turned toward him, her face twisted with emotion. The man was overshadowed by the light of her star. Eventually, Graham leaned in to Ewan and whispered, "Who is she?"

Ewan sent him a side glance and then wrote on his pad for a moment. When he turned it over to Graham, it read, *"Lydia Ford. She's the toast of London theatre at present. The reason why everyone wants to see this play."*

"Lydia," he repeated as he turned the notebook back to his friend. He stared at the lady again. She had turned her face and was looking up at the box, at him, though that was just a trick of the light. He knew she couldn't truly see him in the shadows.

"Beautiful," he whispered.

Next to him, he was aware that Ewan and Tyndale exchanged a look, but he didn't care. For the first time in what felt like forever, a heated interest had lit in his chest. A need for a woman. *This* woman. Lydia Ford.

And he wanted to meet her, to see if that desire would last longer than the duration of a play.

Lydia Ford sat on the settee in the dressing room behind the stage, mending a hole in one of her costumes and laughing with her understudy, Melinda Cross.

"I swear, Robin has to stop stabbing me so hard in that death scene," Lydia said as she shook her head. "Even a wooden sword hurts like a bugger and he keeps tearing the gown. Does he do the same to you on the nights when you play the role?"

"He's a clod but no, he's never put a hole in my gown." Melinda rolled her eyes. "I think he's just jealous that everyone comes to see *you* perform, not him."

Pride swelled in Lydia's chest at her friend's compliments, for she was gratified by her nights in the theatre. More to the point, she recognized how lucky she was to be able to do the work, given where she'd come from. Her two worlds couldn't be more different.

There was a light knock on the door and they both turned to see their stage manager, Toby Westin, open it. He was a tall, thin man with a nervous disposition and a sheet of paper covered with a never-ending list of things to do. "Lydia, you have someone who wishes to meet you."

Lydia shook out the gown she'd been repairing before she got to her feet. "Oh?" she asked as she hung the garment. She tried to sound nonchalant, but dread rose in her chest.

One thing she had learned in her few short months as a star of the stage was that men flocked to actresses. Oh, none of them would dare go out in public with one, since any lady who walked the boards was considered hardly better than a whore, but in private they were drawn like moths to a flame.

Even during her short time as an actress she'd had several impertinent offers from merchant and gentleman alike and had turned them all down as kindly as she could manage when her stomach was turning.

"Please tell us it's not that awful Sir Archibald," Melinda interjected with a shudder. "He refuses to leave me alone no matter how often I turn down his disgusting advances."

Lydia gave her friend a supportive glance. No one liked the nasty Sir Archibald. He was a fixture at the theatre and pushed himself where he didn't belong whenever possible. He also grabbed the behinds of any actress he got within arm's length of and made himself a general nuisance whenever he came backstage after a show.

"No," Toby said with a concerned glance for Melinda. "It's most certainly *not* Sir Archibald. *You* have caught the attention of a duke, Lydia."

She swallowed as the room began to spin and her ears started to ring. Using every bit of talent she had, she fought to keep her reaction from her face and gave Toby the smile she knew was expected of her.

"A duke, *really*? How…interesting."

"Interesting?" Melinda crowed. "You mean lucrative."

"Depending on the duke," Lydia corrected her softly. "Who is this man?"

"Northfield," Toby said, raising both eyebrows.

Melinda spun on her, her pretty face lit up with nothing short of glee. "The Duke of Northfield, Lydia, my goodness! You know who he is, don't you?" She didn't wait for the answer before she continued, "He's devilishly handsome for one, and young. *And* rich. He was engaged to some chit and his best friend stole the woman right out from under him. Since then he's been locked away."

Lydia swallowed hard. She knew *all* those things. Though from very different sources than Melinda had heard them. "Where do you get these rumors?" she asked, forcing a laugh past her dry throat.

Melinda grinned. "I, unlike you, care about Society, Lydia. A woman in my position ought to. There are many paths one can take to financial security."

Toby snorted and Lydia paced away as the two began the same argument they had at least once a week about actresses who became mistresses. Despite her aversion to Sir Archibald, Melinda wasn't opposed to becoming an important man's lover. She was always encouraging Lydia to consider the same option.

But Melinda only did that because she didn't know the truth. The truth that Lydia protected jealously and went to great lengths to hide. But now that the Duke of Northfield desired to meet Lydia all her work seemed poised on the edge of a precipice. He could destroy not only this world, but the other one she inhabited on a regular basis because if he was in a room with her he might *see* her. It was one thing to see on stage, from far away, with bright lights making her seem like something she wasn't.

But closer up, Northfield might see the secret she struggled to keep every time she left the stage.

That secret was that she was *not* Lydia Ford. Lydia Ford had no address, no family, no past and no future. Lydia Ford did not exist. She had *never* existed, not for more than a few hours a week at the theatre. She had been made up of whole cloth, a necessity to allow her to do what she liked without fear of recrimination for the real her.

The *real* her. She shut her eyes. Oh, the real her was someone wildly different than the confident, popular actress seen on stage. A woman no one noticed, not even enough to realize she snuck out three times a week to become the city's most celebrated performer.

That person was Lady Adelaide, the wallflower daughter of the long-dead Earl of Longford.

"Are you well?" Melinda asked, cocking her head.

Adelaide jumped. She was slipping if her friend could see her worry. She brightened her smile. "Of course."

"So are you going to meet him?" Toby pressed.

Adelaide stared down at the hands she'd clenched before herself. They shook. How could she get out of this? "I'm not certain it's wise. Why not let him meet Melinda?"

Toby shook his head immediately and his frown deepened. "He was clear about what he wanted and he doesn't seem the kind of man one refuses. He wants to meet *you*, Lydia, and that's all that will satisfy him. I'm not certain he wouldn't just barge in here if I told him no."

Adelaide sighed. Of course, Toby was probably right. She'd been in Society all her life, she'd known many a man of power and privilege. And she'd had plenty of time to observe Northfield, as well, for he was hard to ignore. In a room full of men who were average, he was...*not*. Perhaps it was his piercing blue eyes or the hard edge to his expression or that he rarely danced, even with the lady who had once been his fiancé.

Whatever it was, Toby was correct in his assessment that Northfield *wasn't* the kind who took no for an answer.

She looked at herself in the mirror. She had changed into a plain gown, but she had not yet removed her stage makeup, and her hair was down. She still looked like Lydia rather than plain, mousy Adelaide. Perhaps Northfield wouldn't recognize her.

It wasn't as if he ever talked to her in Society anyway. There, *she* was a gnat and *he* was a god.

"It's a good thing I still look presentable," she said with a sigh. "Yes, of course, allow him to come in."

Toby left to fetch the man and Melinda jumped up. "Oh, Lydia! What a night. Just think, you could advance your fortunes with just a few well-placed words."

Adelaide pursed her lips. "I'm perfectly content with my fortunes as they are, Melinda," she said. "I'm not trying to advance myself."

Melinda stared at her like she'd spoken Latin or grown a second head. "Not advance yourself?"

Adelaide laughed at her friend's confusion. "Gracious, Melinda, did it never occur to you that perhaps I just like walking the boards? That I'm not trying to do anything but enjoy the time I have to do so?"

"Well, to each his own." Melinda shook her head. "But I still say if you don't try to at least flirt with the man, you're wasting your time and a golden opportunity."

Adelaide sighed. "How about this? The moment he realizes I'm nothing but a boring mouse, I'll send him to you."

"Oh, do!" Melinda said on a laugh as there was a second knock on the door. This time it was harder, more confident, and Adelaide's heart sank. It was *him*.

Melinda shot her a final look and then opened the door, revealing the Duke of Northfield. And as she stared at him, trying not to reveal too much, trying not to fall over from nervousness, Adelaide's heart all but stopped.

CHAPTER TWO

Adelaide stared as the Duke of Northfield ducked beneath the low doorframe and stepped into her dressing room. Suddenly the chamber felt tiny because he filled the space so completely. He was...*beautiful*. That was the only way to describe a man as put together as the one who stood before her. A tall, broad-shouldered Adonis with blond hair that was pulled back in a queue because it was too long for current fashion, a scruffy slash of facial hair across a well-defined jaw, and blue eyes that were the color of a cloudless sky.

He looked across the room at her. Their eyes met and she could think of nothing, do nothing, be *nothing* except a speechless fool as he stared at her.

Melinda, on the other hand, had no such problem. She let out a low curtsey. "Your Grace," she said, her tone filled with the kind of theatric deference that they normally reserved for performances of Shakespeare's works.

Northfield darted his gaze to Adelaide's understudy, though he showed no interest in the pretty brunette. "Good evening."

"Melinda Cross, Your Grace," Melinda cooed, edging herself closer and batting her eyelashes seductively. "I'm Mrs. Ford's understudy."

"*Mrs.* Ford," Northfield repeated, his eyebrows lifting.

Adelaide somehow kept her expression calm. The actresses all labeled themselves as Mrs. It was the best way to maintain a modicum of safety and decorum in a profession that was looked down upon by their so-called betters.

"Good evening, Your Grace," Adelaide said, moving forward at last. "I'm Lydia Ford."

"Yes, I know," Northfield said, a tiny smirk tilting up one corner of his full lips.

Great God, why did her brain have to point out that they were full? Now all she could do was stare at them. And he certainly never had *that* look on his face when he was in ballrooms being proper and…skulky. Was skulky a word? She didn't even know anymore. Either way, he looked…*wicked* right now.

Melinda looked between them slowly and then sighed. "Well, I can see where I'm not wanted. Good evening, you two."

"Don't shut the—" Adelaide began, but Melinda slipped from the room and closed them in together. "—door."

Northfield tilted his head. "Don't want to be alone with me?"

Adelaide took a long breath and thought briefly of her first night on the stage. She'd been just as petrified as she was now and it had gone well. Thus far Northfield had made no indication that he recognized her true identity. All she had to do was present herself in the way he expected and she would be fine.

Somehow.

"We've only just met," she said, stunned by how husky her voice sounded. That fact would help her, of course, for it was a bit different than her normal tone. But why did her throat feel so thick? "Do you think it's proper for us to be alone together?"

He seemed to consider the question. "Perhaps not. But I've been proper for a long time and it's gotten me…"

He trailed off, and for a brief moment she saw a flash of emotion over his face. A flash of regret and pain and anger that touched her soul. She knew all those emotions very well, herself, and considering what he'd been through lately, she believed he had every right to them.

But she wasn't meant to know those things, gossip or not.

So she smiled. "What has it gotten you?"

"Nothing," he finished with a small shake of his head. "Nothing good, at any rate."

She shivered at how close the room felt and turned away to give herself some space, at least in her crowded brain. "Why did you want to meet me, Your Grace?"

He chuckled. "I imagine I'm not the first man who has come to your dressing room to talk to you after a show."

She glanced over her shoulder at him and caught her breath once more at how handsome he was. This was getting ridiculous. "It would be a lie to say you were."

"And you don't lie?" he asked, his gaze narrowing.

She faced him. There was such an edge to his voice. To his body language. A tension and a coiled strength that felt very…dangerous. And yet she didn't want to step away from it.

"I try very hard not to," she said, even though that was a falsehood in itself.

Right now her entire persona was a lie. Lydia Ford, the actress this man was…well, it felt like he was stalking her across the room. Every time she edged back, he moved forward, and it was very distracting. But he was stalking *Lydia*, and Lydia only existed for a few hours each week and then she was packed away like the costumes Adelaide wore and the lines she spoke.

"You're blushing," Northfield said with another half-smile. "Do I make you nervous?"

She swallowed and pushed her shoulders back slightly. "You do, for I'm still not certain why you are here, Your Grace."

"Ah," he said, folding his arms and making his broad chest even more noticeable. "Well, I can remedy that. I came to congratulate you on a good show."

She tilted her head. In Society she might be viewed as an innocent lady, but that was as much of a mask as Lydia was. Adelaide was no fool and she knew the reason why men came in the back to talk to actresses.

"You thought I was good, did you?" she said, arching a brow.

"You sound like you don't believe me," Northfield said with a chuckle.

She shrugged. "What was your favorite line of mine? What did you think I delivered especially well?"

He met her gaze and she saw that he recognized she was calling his bluff. To her surprise, he leaned in. "My favorite line was when you said, 'We are all walking through this world as shadows, ghosts. Some of us just hide it better.'" He gave her a look and then stepped back. "You also died very prettily."

Despite herself, Adelaide laughed at his words, and his face lit up like he'd won something. It was funny, for she'd known of this man for most of her adult life. He and his friends, all dukes, all members of some exclusive little club, were impossible to ignore. Hell, her own best friend Emma had just married one of them less than six months before.

But she'd never *known* Northfield. Just been intimidated by him. Now she found herself liking him. It was impossible not to when his rare smile made him even more handsome.

"Very well, so you *were* paying attention to the play," she said. "You must forgive me for doubting you, for most men who come back to compliment me couldn't even tell me what the performance was about. They come to…"

"Seduce you?" Northfield supplied, and the smile fell, replaced by a look that could only be called smoldering. The man was *smoldering* at her, and the spot between her legs began to tingle even though she didn't want it to.

"Yes," she gasped out.

He inched forward, closing the distance he had allowed and nearly touching her with his big body.

"Do not mistake me, Mrs. Ford, I absolutely came back here to seduce you."

Adelaide squeaked. She didn't mean to squeak, but the sound escaped her lips before she realized it was going to happen or could call it back. But how could she not? Northfield was standing right against her, his body brushing hers in a most inappropriate fashion, crowding her against her makeup table and he just…took all the air out of the room. Out of her lungs. He took all protests out of her brain when he was this close.

All those reactions made it very clear to her that she had been far more than just intimidated by him during the years she'd watched him roam through Society. She'd been attracted to him. But while a man like Graham Everly, rich and popular Duke of Northfield, might not look twice at Adelaide Longford, spinster daughter of a minor and very dead earl, he was looking more than enough at Lydia Ford.

And right now she liked being Lydia Ford more than she ever had before.

"Do you think you could?" she whispered, shocked by the flirtatious words that fell easily from her lips. "Succeed where all other men who have come back here have failed?"

He smiled again. "Ah, a challenge. I've always…*risen* to a challenge, Mrs. Ford. Lydia."

Her hands were shaking, and she reached back to steady herself on the table behind her so he wouldn't see. Tonight she was Lydia, a character she had created so she could do what she wished. And Lydia was bold and confident where Adelaide wasn't. She had to *be* Lydia. What harm was there in it, anyway? This was just a passing fancy of his. They'd flirt and that would be the end of it.

Except he wasn't talking or flirting anymore. He was moving forward and suddenly one of his massive, muscular thighs pushed against her skirts, then farther forward. His chest brushed hers. He reached out and slid his hand along her jawline, up into her hair. It was the first time he'd ever touched her, and she was shocked at the tingling heat that shot from his fingertips and through her entire trembling body.

He tilted her head back, forcing her to look up and up into his handsome face. "I'm going to kiss you, Lydia," he promised, his mouth moving toward hers. "Unless you tell me not to."

Adelaide swallowed hard. She should say no. She was going to, because that was what was proper, *right*. Because she already knew the consequences of giving in to desires, of forgetting oneself.

Except her mouth just couldn't form the words. Her body couldn't pull away. She stood there, silent and staring, watching as this man's full lips descended upon hers. And then he was kissing her.

At first it was just a brush of lips, tender, even a bit tentative. His beard was soft against her chin. Her eyes fluttered shut and she stopped thinking, stopped bargaining with herself, stopped fighting between Adelaide and Lydia. But then the pressure of his mouth increased, his hand angled her head slightly and she caught her breath as his lips parted.

He took advantage of that and his tongue glided past her lips. The world evaporated. She lifted her hands to his upper arms, clinging to his biceps as she heard herself let out a low, hungry sound of pleasure.

And there *was* pleasure. This man knew how to kiss. He drove his tongue inside of her mouth, stroking her own, building a fire of passion that she rarely allowed to burn because it frightened her. But there it was, exploding out of control as he slid a hand around her waist and drew her up hard against the unyielding plane of his big body.

She let her tongue tangle with his as that fire pulsed through her veins, cascading down her limbs, settling heat at her hard nipples, at her tingling sex, at her shaking knees.

He made a harsh groan in the back of his throat as he lifted her onto the table behind her, setting her bottom on the edge and leaning into her with all his weight. She dug her fingers into his shoulders as she reveled in that sound. It was a sound of surrender, of being swept away.

The Duke of Northfield was being swept away by *her*.

And she was not far behind him. He used his thigh to part her legs and stepped between them, tangling her gown and letting her feel the harsh, insistent thrust of his erection against her belly. Her eyes went wide as he continued kissing her, for he was a large man in all ways.

His hands began to move and her mind emptied again. He

cupped her hip, then slid his fingers up her side until he brushed her breast with the tips. She arched against him, sensation mobbing her as he flicked her sensitive nipple with his thumb.

He smiled against her mouth and drew back, their panting breaths matching in the quiet room. He held her gaze, forcing her to drown in seaside blue, as he rolled his thumb around and around the nub. Electric pleasure, hot and heavy, ricocheted through her body and she let out a low cry as she jolted against him in helpless pleasure.

Her entire body throbbed, wetness flooded her sex, her legs shook until she feared they wouldn't support her if she was forced to stand on her own. This man did these things, easily. And it was clear he wanted more.

What was even clearer was that she would allow him to take more. She would surrender to his ministrations because desire drove inside her like a persistent drumbeat. And she was helpless to it, to him, in a way she had never experienced before.

He lowered his mouth again and just before he could kiss her, there was a knock at the door behind them.

They both froze, locking eyes, and slowly he backed away from her. He held out a hand and she took it to get off the table. She smoothed her tangled skirt, her cheeks flaming as reality intruded upon this wild and wanton fantasy she'd been playing out.

"Yes?" she called out, her voice thick and rough from desire and pleasure.

Toby popped his head into the room once more and jolted as he saw Adelaide and Northfield standing together in the middle of the room. "I'm sorry, Lydia, I didn't know you still had a visitor," he said, darting his gaze down to the ground. "Richard wants to know if you plan to perform on Tuesday."

Adelaide swallowed, trying to refocus her kiss-addled mind. She normally did a show on Saturday and two during the week, assuming she could get away. Most actresses weren't allowed that kind of independence to choose their schedule, but her popularity had afforded her some freedom. A good thing, too, since it was a mighty trouble to escape her home and the watching eyes of her guardian aunt.

"Y-Yes," she breathed. "Tuesday."

"Good," Toby said, making a note on a piece of paper. "Well, I'll...I'll see you then. Goodnight, Lydia."

She nodded, and he shot her one last look as he closed the door again. Adelaide felt Northfield watching her as she moved away from him. Felt the heat of that stare and the promises it held. And a great part of her wanted to fall right back into the place they'd been when they were interrupted.

But reality had returned, not just the reality of where they were and the position they were in...but the reality of who she really was. She couldn't surrender to passion with the Duke of Northfield. That was foolish to even consider.

"You are frowning," Northfield said, his voice low and seductive.

She glanced at him over her shoulder and her heart stuttered. God, but she wanted to turn back into him, lift herself against his chest and throw all caution to the wind. But she shoved that wicked part of herself aside and shook her head.

"I'm only remembering reality, Your Grace. And where I am."

He cocked his head. "If where you are is a problem, I have a solution."

She faced him slowly. "And what is that?"

"Come back to my home," he suggested. "And let's continue what we started."

She hesitated. What he was offering was shocking to Lady Adelaide, proper Society miss. He never would have thought to say such a thing to *her*. But to actress Lydia Ford? Well, why wouldn't he offer a night of sin and passion? How many actresses in her acquaintance were having affairs with men like him?

But she *wasn't* Lydia, not really. And surrendering to this passion he offered her was dangerous to her real life. So she shook her head even though it took a great deal of effort to do so.

"I-I don't think so, Your Grace," she whispered. "I was carried away a moment ago, but my level head has returned and I-I think it would be best if I simply offer you my thanks for your compliments on my performance and say good night."

His eyes went wide, like he was surprised at her answer, and she held her breath as she waited for him to grow angry with her. To push, like so many did when they didn't get what they wanted. The Sir Archibalds of the world used their power to leverage control, certainly the Duke of Northfield had far more to leverage than most.

But instead his mouth turned up into one of those fetching half-smiles and he nodded. "Very well, Lydia. I shall bid you good night. For now. But I think we both know that we have unfinished business." He stepped toward the door and opened it, letting the air back into the room. He nodded at her. "I very much look forward to our next encounter."

Then he was gone, leaving Adelaide to sag against the table where he had all but ravished her. Leaving her to ponder his words. Their next encounter might not be where the duke would expect it. And she could only hope that this night wouldn't bring down all she had carefully built to protect herself.

CHAPTER THREE

Graham looked around the room at the spinning couples in their finery and barely held back a sigh. He had not been to a ball in months, not since the betrayal that had sent him spiraling into himself. Now he felt uncomfortable, especially since it seemed the whole room was determined to stare at him. Judging. Whispering.

Tyndale stepped up beside him and held out a drink. "Here, to buoy your strength."

Graham shook his head. "I doubt a watered down drink will buoy anything," he said, though he took the offering before he looked out into the crowd again. "I don't want to be here."

Tyndale turned toward him, genuine kindness and understanding in his dark green eyes. "I know, mate. I really do. After Angelica died, coming back to Society was torture. The loss was still fresh and the whispers magnified it. But I promise you it will get easier the more you do it."

Graham flinched. "It must make you sick to hear me whine about Simon and Meg when compared to your loss."

Tyndale's forehead wrinkled and he reached out to squeeze Graham's arm. "Pain isn't a competition. You have a right to the feelings in your heart. I just don't want to see you drown in them."

Together they looked around the room again and for a moment both were quiet. Then Tyndale glanced at him from the corner of his eye. "Why did you decide to come out tonight?"

Graham shifted. The answer to that was unexpected and complicated. After his impulsive and highly passionate encounter with Lydia Ford at the theatre, life had seemed a little less...grim. And when Tyndale had pushed him to come to the ball, the invitation had seemed less horrifying than it had the first twenty times he'd been asked to return to Society by a well-meaning friend.

"It just felt like time," he said on a sigh. "I can't hide forever, can I?"

Tyndale was about to answer, it seemed, when there was a buzz of commotion at the ballroom entrance. Both men turned toward it, and everything in Graham's world slowed to half-time. A couple had entered the space and the butler was announcing them to the room.

"The Duke and Duchess of Crestwood," the voice came.

Graham stared as Simon and Meg entered the room. Simon was smiling, that bright, mischievous grin he'd had since the first moment Graham met him. Light to his own darkness when they were boys. His chest hurt as every happy memory they'd shared bombarded him, reminding him of how close they'd been. Making him wish they could be close again, even though Simon's betrayal still stung.

Meg clung to Simon's arm, her face lit up with pure happiness. He hadn't seen his former fiancée since the day they had ended their engagement and he left her brother James's home for London.

He hadn't seen Simon since a short time after that, when they'd nearly come to blows at White's.

"Christ," Tyndale muttered, interrupting his thoughts. "I'm sorry, Northfield, I had no idea they'd be here tonight."

Graham swallowed hard past a thick throat. There was a huge part of him that wanted to bolt from the room. But he felt all the eyes of what seemed like the world on him in that moment. The room was watching with more focus and whispering with even more volume than they had when they realized he had come to the party.

If he left…well, that would multiply this scandal that had been caused by Simon and Meg's imprudence. All of them would suffer for it.

In that moment, Simon looked across the room and met Graham's eyes. His friend's face lit with shock, with pain and with regret, and Graham's stomach turned. He didn't want to talk to Simon. Not here. Not now. Not yet.

"I have to…I have to move," Graham muttered, more to himself than to Tyndale. He didn't wait for his friend's reply, but took off through the crowd, blindly reaching for escape from the situation and the feelings it evoked in him.

He had to find something to do, something to busy himself so he wouldn't be bothered, approached, questioned, revealed. And as he edged around the dancefloor, it occurred to him.

He'd dance. He rarely did so, he'd never enjoyed the endeavor, but he was capable of it. And if he were dancing, then he couldn't be bothered.

But the trick was finding the right partner. He scanned the watching faces around the edge of the ballroom. Most of the women were on the hunt, looking for husbands or a rich mine of gossip. Dancing with one of them would not make the situation better, but worse, for he was certain they would try to comfort him, prod him and lure him.

He didn't wish to be lured. Just danced with silently.

So he turned his attention to the wallflowers, who were normally in a quiet line along the wall. Tonight, there appeared to be only one lady standing in her spot there, a woman with dark blonde hair pulled back severely in a plain bun. She wore small, dark-rimmed spectacles and a gown with a high neckline and a shapeless quality.

Lady…God, what was her name? His addled mind searched for it, searched for it and finally found it.

Adelaide. He would dance with Lady Adelaide. Certainly no harm could come of that. So he focused his attention and stalked toward her.

Adelaide had been watching the societal drama play out before her with a level of horror and empathy that made her chest hurt. At first when she'd seen Northfield enter the ballroom with the Duke of Tyndale, she had panicked. His return to Society so soon after their encounter at the theatre had felt anything but coincidental, and she'd been terrified he might have realized who she really was and come here looking for her.

Swiftly she'd realized he wasn't looking for anyone, certainly not her. She'd felt disappointment as well as relief at that realization. But there had also been a small part of her that was *proud* of the man.

Returning to the whispers of the crowd couldn't be easy, but he was facing it. And then the Duke and Duchess of Crestwood had entered the room and everything had come crashing down. People had started talking, staring, and then the two men had looked at each other and…

God, it was just so hard to watch. She'd wanted to rush up to Northfield and comfort him, somehow. To draw him away from the pain this blasted situation was obviously causing him. She hadn't, of course, for it wasn't her place. Northfield didn't want her, he wanted an illusion. He wanted Lydia. And she didn't want to muddy the lines between herself and the character she'd created.

So when he'd turned to come across the room and suddenly his gaze focused on her, it was like the world had screeched to a halt. His eyes were so bright and he had tamed his long hair back in a queue and trimmed his beard, though not shaved it. He was…glorious. And now he was almost with her and it was becoming less and less likely that she wasn't his target in the room.

"Oh God," she murmured as he reached her. "*Merde.*"

He stopped and smiled down at her, but it wasn't one of those sensual half-smirks he'd given to Lydia two nights before.

No, this was something false and forced, and he didn't even meet her eyes. But God, how he smelled good. Like leather. He wasn't even wearing leather.

"Good evening, Lady Adelaide," he said.

She swallowed at the sound of his deep voice. It reminded her once again of those stolen moments in her dressing room, and all she could think of was his body moving against hers.

"Y-Your Grace," she managed to squeak out.

His gaze narrowed as he looked at her face, and her heart stopped beating. Had he recognized her voice? Was he figuring her out right this very moment?

But then he shook his head and said, "I have come to ask you for a dance, my lady. If your card isn't full."

She stared up at him, with his false smiles and his overly solicitous tone. Everything about what he was asking now was... artificial. He didn't want her. He wanted a way to escape and he saw her, a wallflower, as the easiest way to do that.

He was using her. Annoyance flared in her chest as she folded her arms. "Why?"

He sputtered at her response and said, "Wh-*why*?"

She nodded slowly. "Yes, why?"

He peeked over his shoulder at the Duke and Duchess of Crestwood. They were standing now with the Duke and Duchess of Abernathe. The duchess, Emma, was one of Adelaide's closest friends, and Adelaide could see the concern on Emma's face. They were all talking very closely and very obviously about Northfield.

"Because," Northfield said, and then his countenance changed. The counterfeit pleasantness faded and was replaced by something more real. "Because I have the world staring, my lady. And I can't run out of this room if I ever desire to return to it."

Her lips parted at the pure honesty of that response. It softened the edge of her irritation and she reached out a hand. "Very well," she said. "I would be happy to dance with you, Your Grace."

Relief cascaded over his features like a waterfall and he took her hand to guide her to the dancefloor. Electric awareness jolted through her when he touched her, even though it was through two pairs of gloves. She thought again of being in his arms, kissed thoroughly, his big body hard and insistent and—

He cleared his throat as the music began, and she shook the thoughts away as best she could to focus on the steps. They moved together for a while in silence, coming in to each other, then away, for it was an elaborate country dance he'd chosen to participate in. He moved with grace and confidence, and she found herself looking at him from the corner of her eye.

"You're good at this," she said at last, unable to keep her tongue.

He moved in toward her, touching her palm with his as they slid in tandem. Then he swung away so it was just their fingers touching. "You are surprised?" he asked.

She shrugged one shoulder, keeping her eyes forward rather than stealing a half glance at him again. It was almost impossible, for he now drew her in a much deeper way than he ever had before. After all, she knew what he tasted like.

"I am, I admit," she said. "After all, the world knows you do not dance."

"I do not *like* to dance," he corrected as they came face to face again.

His expression was a bit more relaxed now than it had been when he first approached her. She found herself glad of that, for she felt like she was looking at the same man who had talked to her at the theatre. The other, the one who was twisted with discomfort and pain...he was hard to look at. At least without offering him comfort he would not want.

They spun away and came back in rapid succession, and he finished, "That does not mean I wasn't trained to be proficient."

She sighed. "Well, of course you would be perfect at this, just as you are at all things."

The moment the words left her lips, she longed to call them back. Especially when his bright eyes widened and he tilted his head like he was examining her closer. Once again her stomach clenched. Would he recognize her? And if he did, what would he do?

She stepped away, ducking her head as she spun aside, glad for once that the ridiculously complicated steps kept her from being in his arms. Once there, she might lose her head. Once there, her being Lydia might be too clear.

"I am not perfect," he said softly as they moved back together.

He was not looking at her anymore, but off into the crowd. Off toward the Duke and Duchess of Crestwood. She followed his gaze, trying to read it. Trying to understand the pain that was bubbling under the surface, but she couldn't place the source. It could be that he was just humiliated by the circumstances, but it could also be that he had cared, perhaps still cared, for the woman who had thrown him over.

A fact that made her stomach hurt.

He shook his head and his gaze flitted to her again. "You are also a very good dancer, Lady Adelaide," he said.

She smiled and repeated his earlier question. "You are surprised?" His beat of hesitation told her the answer, and she shook her head. "My lack of partners has nothing to do with my skill, Your Grace. I actually like dancing."

There was a moment when surprise crossed his features and she almost laughed at his confusion. Of course he would be confused. With his confidence, he likely couldn't understand her position in the slightest.

"You should do it more often then," he said, proving her point exactly.

Her smile tightened. "It isn't exactly my choice."

Once again his gaze moved away from her, back toward his friends. His mouth thinned, those full lips becoming a line of painful emotion. "No. I suppose not."

She tilted her head, examining him as they became silent again. Now his attention kept returning, over and over to the Crestwood party, his bright eyes becoming duller and duller with each turn of the dance.

And she longed, yet again, to comfort him somehow. Or to pull him out of his fog, at least. It wasn't her place. Even as Lydia, the woman he had all but ravished in a dressing room, it wasn't her place.

But she didn't give a damn about her place in that moment.

"May I ask you a question?"

He jolted, almost as if he had forgotten her being there, and turned his attention back to her. "You may."

She swallowed hard before she asked, "Did you love the Duchess of Crestwood?"

A plethora of emotion crossed his face at that question. First there was shock that she would dare to ask it. Then pain and finally anger. Anger at them. Anger at her. His blue eyes narrowed and he speared her with a look that she had no doubt had frozen the hearts of many an adversary.

"Most would not be so bold or so foolish as to ask me such a thing," he growled.

She supposed the low tone was meant to frighten her, but it only made her think of his sensual words in the theatre a few nights before.

She lifted her chin and fought for the confidence that came so easily when she was Lydia. "Perhaps not, but you have invited me into your dramas by asking me to dance. Now everyone is looking at me as well as you. I cannot help but be curious about what has brought us here."

He held her gaze for a long moment, then pushed away for a few steps of the dance. When he returned to grasp her hand again, his expression had softened.

"No," he said, his voice so low it was almost imperceptible over the music. "I did not love her."

The relief that flooded Adelaide in that moment was far too strong. It felt like someone had taken weights from her shoulders and she was free. But of course she wasn't. This man didn't even recognize her as the one he'd tried to seduce. Even if he did, there were no promises. Just a lusty encounter he likely regretted and would never repeat.

But knowing he didn't love the beautiful woman he kept staring at still brought her ease. She found herself looking at the Crestwood party again. At the duchess, Margaret, especially. No one could deny her beauty. She had a lovely smile and dark, soulful eyes. Ones which held her handsome husband in rapt attention.

There was a connection between them that was powerful, palpable, even across a crowded room. Where Northfield had not loved her, clearly Crestwood did. And she loved him in return.

"They seem happy," Adelaide murmured.

Northfield's hand tightened in hers and his frown drew deep. "Thank you. That's very helpful."

She jerked her face toward his. "I'm simply saying that if you did not love her and he clearly does, perhaps what happened is for the best."

For a moment, his expression remained unreadable. Then, to her surprise, it relaxed again. Like he had been freed, just a fraction, from his troubles.

"You are very bold," he said, though the words weren't an accusation.

She smiled slightly. "Wallflowers have the prerogative."

The corner of his mouth lifted up into a half-grin and her heart stuttered. *That* was the same seductive look he had given her nights ago, when she was Lydia. When he wanted her. Of course, that was entirely impossible in this situation, but she felt the results of it nonetheless.

The music faded and he bowed to her before he took her arm and began to lead her from the floor. "Would you like to take a turn around the veranda?" he asked.

She stumbled at the unexpected question and he steadied her with a brief touch on the small of her back. She drew a few calming breaths before she faced him.

"Still trying to avoid all those eyes?" she asked, feeling them keenly even now.

He arched a brow. "In part."

"And what is the other part?" she whispered, lost in the intensity of his expression. Lost in the desire she still felt for him even if he didn't know who she was or what they'd done.

"I like bold," he said softly.

Her lips parted with surprise. Her inner voice, the intelligent one, screamed at her to refuse him. Reminded her that every moment she spent with this man made it more likely that her secrets would be uncovered. Her life destroyed.

And yet she found herself nodding slowly. "Very well," she agreed.

He held out his elbow again and she took it, then let him draw her from the ballroom and out into the cool night air.

CHAPTER FOUR

There was one abiding emotion that Graham felt as he escorted Lady Adelaide onto the veranda, and that was utter confusion. Here he had spent the past twenty-four hours ruminating and fantasizing about Lydia Ford. Now he found himself intrigued by this bespectacled wallflower who could not be more different from the confident, sensual actress.

Apparently once he had refilled the well of his desire, it was now overflowing and no woman was safe.

As if she sensed his thoughts, Adelaide edged toward the terrace wall, into the shadows and away from the brighter lights of the house. Almost like she was hiding from him. But why wouldn't she? He knew how he had behaved during their dance.

How *she* had acted was much more surprising.

"You know I am a friend of Emma," she said. "Er, the Duchess of Abernathe."

Graham hesitated. In truth, he had not remembered that detail. He had very rarely thought of the wallflowers at all in the years gone by. Emma hadn't even appeared in his line of sight until she and James began to circle each other. But Graham liked the new duchess, strange and strained a situation as this was.

The fact that Emma counted Adelaide as a friend was more a recommendation of the woman than a condemnation. But he understood why she pointed it out.

"Yes. Does that mean you will be running back to her, reporting everything about our encounter to her?" he asked.

She looked over her shoulder at him, and for a flash of a moment there was an unexpectedly sensual expression on her face. Then she laughed. "No. Most certainly not."

He leaned in, trying to understand why her words, which were bland enough when taken at face value, hit him in the gut the way they did. Made him want to step closer to her. Crowd her a little, just to hear her catch her breath.

It was madness.

"What's your story?" he asked, his tone a little too sharp.

She pivoted now and faced him. Her eyes were wide and she clenched her hands in front of her. "My...my story?"

He folded his arms. "Come now. Everyone has a story. Right now I'm wondering how in the world *you* are a wallflower. You are interesting and intelligent."

She rolled her eyes slightly. "The two hallmarks of a wallflower, Your Grace, you must know that."

He edged forward, just a little. Not enough for his taste, but enough that her eyes widened ever so slightly in the dark. "And lovely," he added, surprised to find that he felt it was true.

Despite her tightly bound hair and ugly dress and the spectacles that blocked him from getting a good view of her eyes, there was something interesting about her slender face. High cheekbones, full lips, a long, lovely neck.

She took a long step away from him and those full lips thinned into a scowl. "What are you doing?"

He blinked. Most ladies would have tittered and cooed over his compliment, but Adelaide actually looked...*angry*.

"Doing?" he repeated, and felt rather stupid for parroting her.

She nodded. "You're playing with me. You've been in ballrooms with me dozens of times and never spared me so much as a glance."

He shifted slightly. "Well, I'm no longer engaged now."

Her brow wrinkled and her hands unclenched in front of her. She stared at him for a beat, two, too long, too close. And then she shocked him by stepping around him and moving back into the ballroom.

"Good night, Your Grace," she tossed over her shoulder, utterly cold and dismissive.

He turned to watch her go, watched her shut the door behind her and leave him alone on the terrace. And he was shocked that what he wanted to do was follow her. Catch her arm. Force her to continue their interaction.

Which was not something he had expected when he chose her to dance with. And it wasn't something he wanted. Not at all.

Adelaide's face felt hot as fire as she reentered the ballroom to the rising whispers of those in attendance. Dozens of pairs of eyes swept to her and most narrowed as they gossiped behind their fans. But it wasn't their chatter that made her dizzy and uncomfortable.

It was Northfield. Damnable Northfield and his intense stare and his lovely smell and the way he could focus on a person and make her feel like she was singular and important and beautiful. Of course she knew something most women in her position wouldn't.

He could do it to *any* woman. After all, just a day before he'd been attempting to seduce Lydia, so how could his flirtation on the terrace with her—Adelaide her, *real* her—mean anything to him? Worse, why did she *want* it to mean anything? This man's interest in her was only dangerous to her double life. The best thing she could do was shrug away from him in both her domains and hope he'd go away forever.

"Adelaide?"

She turned to find Emma, Duchess of Abernathe, approaching her. Adelaide couldn't help but smile, despite her stirred up emotions. She and Emma had been friends for years as they stood along the wall together. And she had hardly seen

Emma for months now, thanks to the duchess's marriage, her pregnancy and the upheaval that had followed.

She stepped forward, hands outstretched, and Emma hugged her tightly, or as tightly as she could manage with her sweet rounded belly in the way.

Adelaide laughed as they parted and let a hand slip to the swell. "You must be going into confinement soon, to await the birth of this ball you're keeping in your belly."

Emma smiled, and she looked so happy that Adelaide hardly recognized her as the warm but worried friend she had counted on for so long.

"Whatever is in there moves around too much now to be a ball," Emma said. "But yes, only a few more events and I will be sliding into my confinement here in London. James insists on that, so I will be close to doctors."

She glanced over her shoulder and Adelaide followed her gaze to the very handsome Duke of Abernathe. He was an intimidating person, for he was the golden child of Society. And yet Emma had not only landed him as a husband, but tempted him into deep and abiding love for her, if his puppy dog expression was any indication.

"The man moons over you," Adelaide whispered. "So the rumors are true."

"Yes," Emma said with a satisfied grin. "I have bewitched him, body and soul, as he has done to me. It's a love match, indeed, and I could not be happier."

Adelaide ignored the twinge of jealousy that momentarily stung her, and squeezed her friend's hand. "No one deserves that more, Emma. No one in the world."

"Well, there's you," Emma suggested. "I'm so happy to see you. And so sorry that with all the rush and commotion of the past few months I haven't been able to see you sooner."

"You know my aunt never would have allowed me to come to Abernathe for your wedding, even if I could have made it in time," Adelaide said with a sigh.

Emma's frown deepened. "She is still the same then."

"Oh, Aunt Opal never changes. She's as predictable as the sun rising and setting each day. She wants me to be out in Society, but she likes how I'm on the fringes. Get too full of myself, as she puts it, and she'll slap me down as soon as pour me tea."

Emma shivered. "But she hasn't actually...*struck* you?"

Adelaide caught her breath. Not that long ago, she and her aunt had gotten into a row, a dreadful one. Over things Emma didn't know. Not her acting career, for her aunt was as in the dark as anyone, but something else. Something harder. More painful. And in the heat of the moment, her aunt had struck her so hard that Adelaide had been forced to cry off parties for two weeks while the bruise around her eye had healed.

Of course Emma had come to call and seen the result of the attack. Her friend had never forgotten that act of violence. Adelaide hadn't fully forgiven it. It had been part of her reckless rebellion that had led her to the stage.

"No," Adelaide said softly. "Not since that one time."

Emma let out her breath on a sigh. Then she linked arms with Adelaide. "Will you come and meet my family, then?" she asked. "I so want you to like them as much as I do."

"Certainly," Adelaide said, letting her friend draw her toward Abernathe. But then her breath caught. Standing with the man were the Duke and Duchess of Crestwood. She'd thought they'd stepped away, but they seemed to be back. Not that it was surprising. After all, the duchess was Abernathe's sister. Which made her Emma's sister now, too.

Emma drew her up, almost bubbling with excitement as they reached the group. "James, do you remember my friend Lady Adelaide?"

Abernathe turned a broad smile to Adelaide and she couldn't help catching her breath. He was certainly well put together. Not as much as his friend Northfield, but one could not deny that Emma had made a fine catch.

"Lady Adelaide," he said, taking her hand and drawing it to his lips briefly. "How wonderful to see you. My wife speaks so highly of you, I cannot imagine we will be anything but fast friends."

Adelaide smiled, for there was an honesty to this man. He wasn't playing a game—he really wanted to like her, if only to make Emma happy. And since no one had spent much time ever making Emma happy, it pleased Adelaide greatly to see that her love match was *truly* that.

"I look forward to that, Your Grace," she said with a slight nod for him. "After all, we have a great deal in common thanks to our shared love of Emma."

Emma blushed and waved at them with one fluttering hand. "Gracious, you'll swell my head as large as my stomach with such talk. Adelaide, may I also present to you my brother and sister-in-law, the Duke and Duchess of Crestwood."

Adelaide turned slowly to the two people she'd been trying to ignore and found herself looking into two smiling, rather kind faces. The Duke of Crestwood was handsome, with blue eyes that were darker than Northfield's and a mischievous air. But he was not the main focus of her attention. Adelaide took in the duchess more closely.

Margaret was lovely. No one could say she wasn't lovely. With dark hair that had lighter highlights, deep brown eyes, and a lithe, lovely figure, there was no doubt why the woman had been the center of Society for so long. But when Adelaide looked at her, all she could see was Northfield's handsome face, twisted with that twinge of pain and betrayal when the two entered the room.

And a strong dislike shot through Adelaide at that memory.

"Lady Adelaide," the duchess said, reaching out a hand to greet her. "I'm so pleased to make your acquaintance. Emma speaks so highly of you, I feel as though I already know you."

Adelaide took the duchess's hand with reluctance and shook it briefly. "Your Grace," she said, her tone cool.

If the duchess sensed her withdrawal, she made no indication. Adelaide was next greeted by the duke, who was as friendly as his wife. She knew under normal circumstances she would have liked them both.

But in that moment, she felt...hesitant. No, not *hesitant*. That wasn't the right word at all. What she felt was protective. Of Northfield. A man she hardly knew and one who didn't give a whit about her.

It was ludicrous.

The group chatted for a moment, about meaningless things. But Adelaide couldn't help her stare slipping back to Margaret again and again. And she noticed the duchess looked at her, too, more than anyone else. Perhaps because she was the newest addition to their circle. Perhaps because she'd noticed Adelaide dancing earlier with her former fiancé.

Not that the woman had any right to feelings on the subject.

With a frown, Adelaide turned her attention back to Emma and was about to ask her about her beautiful gown when there was the sound of a throat clearing behind her. "Adelaide."

Adelaide stiffened at her aunt's voice, saying her name in the same icy tone she'd been saying it for a decade and a half, since her parents died and Aunt Opal had been forced to take her in.

She glanced at Emma, finding her friend smiling with encouragement at her, and slowly turned. "Aunt Opal," she said with false lightness. "There you are. May I introduce you to the Duke of Abernathe, Emma's new husband, and his brother-in-law and sister, the Duke and Duchess of Crestwood."

Her aunt nodded vaguely at the group. "Good evening. And good night, for I'm afraid it is time for Adelaide and me to go."

Adelaide's lips parted. It was not even ten yet, the party would go on for at least a few hours more. Of course, her aunt didn't care. Opal often got it into her head that the night was over and there was no arguing.

Emma stepped forward before Adelaide could respond. "Oh, Lady Opal, could we not persuade you to allow Adelaide to stay? This is the first time I've seen her in an age and I so want to catch up. My husband and I would happily stand in your stead as chaperones and take her home once the night was over."

Opal looked Emma up and down slowly, and Adelaide tensed. Her aunt was capable of behaving very strangely, which Emma knew, but which could also damage Adelaide's position in Abernathe's eyes, or the eyes of the Crestwoods.

"I'm not certain I would trust *you* as chaperone, Emma," Opal said softly, and let her gaze slip first to Abernathe, then to Margaret and her husband.

Adelaide gasped. "Aunt Opal!" she burst out, sending Emma an apologetic look. She could hardly stand to look at James or his family, for she could already see his outraged expression and the shock on the faces of the Duke and Duchess of Crestwood.

"I beg your pardon, madam?" James said, just as softly as Aunt Opal had, but with a dangerous undercurrent that spoke of all the power this man had to wield if he chose to.

Emma reached back and gently touched his arm before she said, "I would never let Adelaide come to any grief. I believe you know that, my lady."

"Perhaps you wouldn't at that," Opal said with a shrug, the cruelty gone from her voice. Whether that was because she feared the subtle strength of Abernathe or because she had simply vented all of it already, Adelaide couldn't say. "Still, our night is over. You will have plenty of time to catch up with Adelaide in the coming weeks, as I hear you will spend your confinement in the city. Good evening."

Opal caught Adelaide's arm and guided her none too gently away from her friends. Adelaide gave Emma an apologetic look as she called out, "Good night!"

She shrugged out of her aunt's grasp as they made their way across the room together and glared at her. "Why in the world did you make a scene with my friends?"

Opal said nothing as she exited into the foyer and signaled to a footman. She was just as silent as they awaited the carriage and were eventually helped into the vehicle that would take them home. Only when they were alone together did her aunt fold her arms and glare at Adelaide.

"You speak of *me* making scenes? I turn my back on you for ten minutes and you create one of your own."

Adelaide pressed her lips together. "Are you talking about me dancing with the Duke of Northfield?"

"Dancing would have been bad enough," Opal said with a snort of disgust. "That man is dragging scandal behind him like it's chained to his legs. But what I was referring to was your going out onto a terrace alone with him."

Adelaide's lips parted. "Aunt Opal, I merely took a breath of air with him. It is not uncommon for a pair to take a turn on the terrace together."

She did not, of course, add that she had been attracted to Northfield. Nor that she had lost herself to wild abandon with him in a dressing room. Her aunt would likely do more than strike her if she knew those bitter truths.

"But *you* are not a common woman," Opal hissed. "We already know you have no ability to control your wanton ways. It's in your very blood. A man like Northfield must be able to sniff that out on you."

Adelaide's chest tightened. "That was a long time ago, Aunt Opal."

Opal turned her face away and looked out the carriage window into the darkness of the street. "Once a wanton, always a wanton," she hissed.

Adelaide flopped back against the seat and shut her eyes. "What do you want from me?" she asked. "If I'm such a disappointment, why push me to continue in Society? It's like a tightrope with you. Not too much, not too little. I hardly know how to satisfy you."

Opal glared at her but didn't reply, and sank into one of her infamous silent treatments. Adelaide sighed, but in truth she welcomed the coldness. It was better than being railed at. Than being reminded of heartbreaks long past. Of wanton impulses that seemed to be reborn when she was around Northfield.

And perhaps that was the best reason of all to avoid him from now on.

CHAPTER FIVE

When Emma glided through the parlor door the next day, Adelaide couldn't help but smile widely. The two women embraced and then took their places for tea, and for a moment it felt like nothing had changed between them.

Except that Emma's pregnant belly and Adelaide's wandering mind made it clear that a great deal had. Soon it seemed there was no avoiding that fact, for after a while Emma set her cup down and speared her with an appraising look.

"We've talked enough about me and my new life," she said. "I want to talk about *you*."

Adelaide shifted. "What is there to talk about? While you went off and fell in love, I have been here in London, doing as I always do. I'm quite predictable, you know."

Emma arched a delicate brow. "Are you? I don't think you are. As long as I've known you, I have always suspected your still waters ran very deep, indeed."

Adelaide held back a laugh. If only Emma knew the truth, she would be shocked. How many times had Adelaide thought to tell her about how she had turned to the theatre, about what had driven her there...even now she wanted to talk to her about Northfield, get her insider information about the man.

She did none of those things. "You are too adorable, my friend," Adelaide insisted, though she kept her gaze away from Emma's. "To think I might have secrets that I could keep from you."

"I saw you dancing with Graham last night," Emma said softly.

Graham. Adelaide stopped short at the use of his Christian name. It was safer to think of him as Northfield. Northfield was a title, a dukedom, it meant distance. Almost like he wasn't...*real.* Graham was a person. A man. A man with full lips that tasted of sherry, with strong arms and with a brokenness that she couldn't help but want to fix, even though it wasn't her place in either of her double lives.

"Adelaide?"

Adelaide blinked, shrugging off her thoughts as best she could. "The room at large saw me dancing with Northfield," she said. "What could I do when he asked? Refusing would have been so rude."

Emma hesitated. "Do you know him?"

"No," Adelaide said swiftly. "Not really at all. I mean, I've seen him. We always saw those men in that club that your husband lords over."

Emma's smile softened. "The 1797 Club," she clarified. "A brotherhood of dukes with very bad fathers."

Adelaide frowned. "Not much of a brotherhood considering what Crestwood did to Northfield."

Emma stiffened, and Adelaide immediately wished she could snatch the words back. They felt too emotional, and they were her rushing to the defense of a man she had just claimed she knew nothing about.

She focused on refreshing their cups of tea. "Or so gossips say," she added.

Emma shook her head. "It is so much more complicated than gossip says, I assure you. It's an unfortunate situation, of course, and Graham is very much entitled to his feelings."

"I should say so," Adelaide grumbled, her mind turning once again to the desperation on his face when he'd asked her to dance the night before.

Emma arched a brow and continued, "But Meg and Simon

are very sorry for the circumstances. They almost lost their chance at happiness in some bid to make up for what they did."

Adelaide wrinkled her brow. Seeing them so happy the night before, it was hard to picture Northfield's suffering keeping them up at night. But Emma seemed adamant and she had never been one to lie. It wasn't in her nature.

"I'm sure I don't know anything about it," Adelaide said with a wave of her hand. "And I doubt I shall spent any time with Northfield again, so it is really none of my business."

"Is that why you don't like Meg?" Emma pressed.

Adelaide had taken a sip of tea and she nearly spit it out across the room. She wiped her mouth as she tried to regain some composure.

"Not like the Duchess of Crestwood?" she repeated. "Why in the world would you think that?"

Emma leaned in. "Because I know you, best friend of mine. I can see when you are false and when you are true. You were odd last night with her." She shook her head. "Come to think of it, you've been odd a great deal lately. Even before I married. Is there anything you want to tell me?"

Once again Adelaide considered confessing all she had to hide to her friend, but decided against it. It was too high a risk. "Of course not." She sought a change of subject and found it. Though it was not a topic that pleased her as she said, "I'm sorry my aunt was so wretched to you last night."

Emma shrugged. "I could care a fig about what your aunt Opal says to me."

"Your Abernathe looked as though he wished to call her out," Adelaide said with a shake of her head. "Pistols at dawn with my spinster aunt."

"He's protective," Emma said with a smile. "But I don't need it. *You* do. Was she very hard on you after?"

Adelaide shrugged. "Just harsh. You know her and her erratic behavior."

Emma frowned. "You could come and stay with James and me," she suggested.

40

"She'd never allow it," Adelaide said immediately. "At any rate, I'm…fine. I'm fine."

Emma didn't look convinced. "Well, what about just joining us for supper? Do you think Opal would allow for that?"

Adelaide considered it. She would not return to the theatre for another performance until the next night. "I think I could convince her," she said. "If my maid was with me as chaperone."

Emma's face lit up. "Wonderful. I so want you to see our home and the nursery and get to know James better."

Adelaide couldn't help but beam at Emma's enthusiasm. "Well, my dear, I look forward to all that, too. It will be nice to have a night away where I can just be myself and not worry about anything but how much dessert to eat."

"Your Grace?"

Graham looked up from his ledger to find his butler, Rogers, standing at the door to his study. The man had been with his father and continued on after the previous Northfield's death nearly eight years before. Because of their long acquaintance, Graham knew the servant could read his troubles, probably better than most.

Graham could do the same. From the way the older man kept shifting his weight, he could see whatever Rogers was about to say was not pleasant.

"What is it?" Graham asked, carefully setting his quill down and focusing his attention as best he could. A difficult feat considering his head had been spinning for days now.

"You have a visitor," Rogers said softly. "The Duke of Abernathe."

Graham froze. Although his quarrel was with Simon, his relationship with James had been strained for months. Not strained—destroyed. Before the ball the previous night, he hadn't seen the man he'd considered his brother since he walked out of his home in the country months before.

"I see," he said, rising. "I assume he will not be turned back?"

A hint of a smile crossed over Rogers face. "You know the duke, sir. He's always been quite singular."

"Stubborn as an ass," Graham corrected. "Yes, I know. Well, show him in."

Rogers seemed pleased at Graham's response and stepped out to fetch his guest. That gave Graham a moment's reprieve before he faced what was about to come. He smoothed his waistcoat and shook out his suddenly tingling hands.

And then James walked into the room slowly. He paused at the doorway, and Graham stared at him. His friend looked lighter than he ever had, happier thanks to his recent marriage. The concern in his eyes was only for his friend, not for his own troubles.

Graham couldn't help but be happy for that fact. He knew his friend deserved the happiness he'd found.

"Graham," James said at last. "I admit I feared you would not see me."

Graham cleared his throat. "Is that why you haven't called before?"

James shifted. "After our last encounter, I thought it best to give you your space. I knew you were well, or at least as well as could be expected because of—"

"Your spies," Graham grunted. When James seemed surprised, he laughed softly. "Oh yes, I know Ewan and Matthew and even Kit report back to you when they see me. You're our fearless leader, after all. King of the Dukes."

James sighed. "Some king. I allowed my kingdom to be destroyed."

Graham shook his head. "That wasn't you, mate. At any rate, I'm..." He hesitated, then met James's eyes. "I'm happy to see you," he admitted.

James's expression softened and he crossed the room, hand outstretched. "I'm so happy to see you."

Graham stared at the hand, then grabbed it and tugged James in for a brief hug. He pounded James's back and backed away, both men shifting from the discomfort of the emotional display.

"Drink?" Graham asked, turning away to regain some control over his emotions.

"Yes." James's voice was thick.

Graham poured them each a scotch and motioned to the chairs by the fire. They sat together, nursing the drinks for a moment before James set his aside and leaned forward, draping his forearms over his knees.

"Does your accepting me here mean you have decided to forgive your friends?"

Graham closed his eyes. James meant Simon. James meant going back to normal. He'd been thinking of it more and more lately, but seeing Simon the night before made him realize just how much he still stung.

He sighed. "I know it isn't your fault. That this quarrel is between Simon and me, but—"

"Just come to supper," James interrupted.

Graham opened his eyes and stared. His friend looked a little desperate as he made the suggestion. "I don't know," he said slowly.

James shook his head. "It will only be Emma and me," he reassured him. "Please, it's just a start. I only want a start, Graham."

Graham pushed to his feet and paced across the room as he considered the request. He did miss James. He missed all his friends and the camaraderie and family they had represented to him all the years they'd had their club. They were the only family who had ever mattered.

"Very well," he said at last.

James leapt to his feet, and his grin was almost impossible not to return. "Most excellent," he said. "I'm so happy, and I know Emma will be delighted, as well."

Graham tilted his head. "You're content," he said, a

statement, not a question.

"I am more than content. I'm blissful. I never thought I could be so happy, nor deserve to be loved as deeply as she loves me. But I can. I *do*." He stressed the last word heavily. "So do you."

Graham couldn't help but flash to an image of pale blonde hair and soft lips, superimposed over another of dark-rimmed spectacles and sharp wit. He shook the cacophony away and said, "Well, not all of us can be so lucky."

James paused a moment before he said, "You danced with Adelaide last night."

Graham rolled his eyes. "To avoid the whispers of the crowd when Simon and Meg came in. I assure you there was...there was nothing between us."

James pursed his lips. "Well, she is a wallflower. I know from personal experience that wallflowers make the best wives."

Graham waved him off. "For you, perhaps. But right now I assure you that finding a wife is last on a long list of things I want to do."

James shrugged one shoulder. "If you say so. For now I will simply be pleased that one of those things is coming to supper."

"Yes, for now supper will have to be enough," Graham agreed, then elbowed his friend. "Game of billiards?"

James's face lit up. "Absolutely. Since you ran off to London, I haven't had a decent match."

They moved toward the hall together and Graham grinned. "You mean you haven't taught Emma to play yet?" he teased.

James barked out a laugh. "Every time I try, I get...distracted by her," he admitted.

Graham shook his head, even as a warm sense of belonging filled him, one he hadn't allowed for months. Opening this door, even a tiny sliver, felt right to him. And he looked forward to a quiet evening with his friends before he went back to the tangled confusion of his life.

CHAPTER SIX

Adelaide stood in the nursery of Emma's London home, cooing over the sweetest christening outfit she'd ever seen. "The lace is fantastic," she said, fingering the softness of it.

"It's been in James's family for generations," Emma said with a contented sigh. "He wore it, as did Meg, and now this baby will continue the tradition."

"Oh, Emma," Adelaide whispered, shocked that tears suddenly stung her eyes. She turned away so her friend wouldn't see, but turning away from herself was not possible.

She didn't begrudge Emma her happiness, certainly. But she *was* jealous. Despite her sneaking out to act in the theatre, despite her continuing attendance to parties and balls, her life was predictable. Her past wouldn't allow her the future Emma now stepped into.

She would likely live and die alone. She had accepted that fact as best she could. Her escapes were the way she lived with it.

"Adelaide," Emma began, but before she could continue, there were sounds of male voices from the hall.

Adelaide took the distraction, backing from the room as she said, "It sounds as though Abernathe has arrived."

Emma examined her closely but then nodded. "Indeed, it does. Come, let's greet him."

Adelaide followed her friend down to the foyer, gathering

her breath and her senses with every step. She was fine. This was fine. Everything would be fi—

Her mind cut off the soothing thought as she reached the bottom of the stairs and saw that Abernathe was not alone. There, standing beside him as Emma stepped up to greet him, was Northfield.

Graham recognized that Emma was speaking and James was answering, but he had no idea what they were talking about. He was too busy staring at Lady Adelaide. She remained three steps up on the stairs, her hand clenched in a white-knuckled grip on the railing. And she was staring straight at him through those spectacles that made her eyes so frustratingly hard to read. Hard to see at all. All he knew was that they were focused on him.

And he was not sorry about that fact.

"And you know Adelaide, I think, don't you, Graham?"

Graham jolted as Emma placed a warm hand on his forearm and drew his attention back to proper and practical things, like introductions.

"Y-Yes," he croaked, stepping forward to extend a hand. "Lady Adelaide, how nice to see you again."

She swallowed, that slender throat working with the action, and then she came down the last few steps. She stared at his extended hand a beat too long before she took it and allowed him to bow over it briefly.

"I did not know you would be here, Your Grace," she said. Her cheeks brightened to pink the moment she said the words. "I-I mean, good evening."

Emma glanced back and forth between them and then motioned to the room off the foyer. "Gracious, let's not stand in the drafty hall all night. Come, we'll go to the parlor."

She and James led the way and Adelaide fell into step beside Graham as they followed. The moment they entered, she left his side and moved to the opposite end of the chamber, almost as physically far as she could get from him without breaking the glass and hurdling herself out the window and into the street for an escape.

He watched her. She was uncomfortable because of his presence. And of course she would be. Their parting last night had been abrupt, brought on by his compliment of her and her sharp reaction to it.

He hadn't pursued her after that, finding other ways to avoid Simon and Meg before he slipped from the ball with what he hoped was little fanfare. But he'd been thinking of Adelaide ever since, images of her merging and colliding with those of Lydia Ford.

He shook his head when James said, "We'll be right back."

He blinked as Emma and James stepped from the room, leaving him as alone with Adelaide as he had been on the terrace. He shifted his weight. "Where were they going?" he asked. "I'm afraid I wasn't paying attention."

Adelaide speared him with a glance. "They *claimed* to be going to inform the staff that there would be two extra guests for supper. But since either of them could have performed that duty alone or asked a servant to do it, I think they were actually going to talk about the fact that each of them invited one of us without the other knowing."

He tilted his head. "Is that a problem, Adelaide?"

She stiffened at his less formal address of her and turned her face to look out at the dark street below. "It isn't for me, Your Grace."

"Good," he said, and then he did the thing he'd been wanting to do since they entered the room. He took a step toward her.

She wasn't looking at him, but he knew she marked the movement by the way her breath caught and her hand slowly clenched into a fist at her side. Things that only urged him on.

"Last night at the ball, I said something to you that clearly offended you," he said, glancing back at the door to ensure they were not about to be interrupted.

"Of course you didn't," she said softly, refusing to look at him.

"Of course I *did*," he corrected her. "Else you would not have walked away from me on the terrace. I'm not exactly certain how I offended you, but I apologize regardless."

She caught her breath, and now it was she who took a long step toward him. The distance between them was rapidly shrinking, and he found he wasn't sorry for that.

"You aren't *certain*?" she said, keeping her voice low even though the anger in it was clear. "You were toying with me, Your Grace. You were playing a game."

"You accused me of that last night," he said. "And I assure you, I do not play games."

She shook her head. "*All* men play games."

There was something about her tone that drew Graham up short, and he stared at her. For months he had been wrapped up in his own pain and betrayal and heartbreak. He'd been incapable of recognizing anyone else's feelings. Now he saw hers, flitting across that slender face before she packed them away and hid them.

And a strange part of him longed to dig those feelings out. Allow her to express them as she clearly did not do. Comfort her.

He didn't, of course. It wasn't his place. Not in this world or any other. But just because he had no connection to this woman didn't mean he couldn't be gentlemanly. He had the capacity, he just hadn't been in practice lately.

"Adelaide, let me assure you I was not playing a game with you last night. I danced with you because I was uncomfortable with the situation, but I was honest with you about that, wasn't I?"

Her lips parted and his attention was drawn to her mouth immediately. He shook off the reaction as she said, "Well...yes."

"I chose you because I thought you wouldn't hound me

about Meg and Simon. Which, of course, you did."

She gasped in outrage. "I did not!"

He found himself chuckling a little as he shook his head, and was shocked by it. He hadn't laughed in a very long time. "You *did*, Adelaide. But I somehow didn't mind your questions. They're the same ones all my friends have been dancing around for months. You are the first to be so damned direct, and perhaps I needed it in that moment where I felt so…*vulnerable*."

Her brow wrinkled. "Oh."

"And I admit I asked you because I didn't think you'd assume my invitation to take a turn around the dancefloor was an indication that I wished to link my life to yours for the rest of my days."

She clenched her jaw slightly. "Of course not, don't be foolish."

He nodded. "You see, you are practical. I like that about you. Either way, the reason I asked you onto the terrace afterward was because I *did* enjoy the dance and I didn't necessarily wish to stop talking to you. None of that was a game. None of that was a lie."

"But what about what you said on the terrace?" she countered. "You told me you thought I was pretty and I *know* that is a lie. One you probably tell without thinking because it's what simpering, ridiculous fools want you to say when you look into their eyes and pretend to like them."

He shook his head slowly. What the hell had someone done to this woman? Her sharp reaction was too specific not to think it hadn't been born from bitter experience.

"First," he said, ticking one finger with the other. "It isn't a lie. You have an interesting face, Adelaide. Second, I haven't stared into a ridiculous fool's eyes and told her anything for almost a decade. If you recall, I have been engaged up until recently, so I haven't been bent on seducing anyone since I was nineteen." He huffed out his breath. "But if you do not want me to call you pretty, then I will certainly never do so again. I will only compliment you on your intelligence and your wit and the fact that you may be the most frustrating person I have ever had the pleasure of talking to."

He stopped talking for a moment, and his face fell. Great God, what had he just said to this person? This lady? This stranger? And now she was just staring at him, eyes wide beneath her spectacles, face unreadable, but filled with tension.

He opened his mouth to apologize, but before he could, she tilted her head back and began to laugh. The sound took him utterly off guard, for it was a throaty, rich laugh that echoed in the small room around them. A lovely laugh. A sensual laugh, actually.

And a laugh that drew him in and made him smile despite himself.

"Goodness, I'm so sorry," she said as she regained her composure. "I must have seemed like a wretched girl having such a strong reaction to some simple words."

He shook his head. "You didn't. But why *did* you react so strongly?"

She shrugged and the pleasure left her face. "Experience, Your Grace. We all have it, don't we? And sometimes it's impossible not let the past wheedle its way into the present and even damage the future." She moved toward him again, carefully. "But now it seems that you and I are going to see more of each other. I'm so close to Emma, and if you are renewing your friendship with Abernathe we would not be able to avoid it if we wished to. So...so will you allow me to start again?"

He nodded, though he was taken aback by her confidence beneath that shifting wallflower surface. It felt...familiar somehow, though he had no idea why.

"Yes," he said. "I'd like that."

She held out a hand. "Adelaide," she said, as a means to introduce herself.

He stared at her offering and then took it, shaking gently. "Graham," he said, foregoing his title. "At least in private."

"Graham," she said, sliding her fingers from his. "A pleasure to meet you."

Their hosts reentered the room in that moment, and Adelaide blushed as she stepped away from him.

"Well, it's all arranged," Emma said brightly, though her gaze flitted to Adelaide and then slowly to Graham. "I hope you two were able to entertain yourselves."

Graham nodded. "We were, indeed. Your friend is a charming companion."

Adelaide bent her head, and there was a shadow of a smile that tilted her lips, like a private joke had passed between them. And he found he liked that. Liked having her comfortable with him. And that was good, for as she said, they would likely see a great deal of each other if he was renewing his relationship with James and Emma.

And it would be good to have a friend as he figured out where he now fit in his old circle.

Adelaide sipped her after-dinner drink and watched as Graham bent over the billiard table to take a shot. Instead of separating after supper, James had suggested the foursome remain together to talk as the men played their game. Now Adelaide was happy they had done so, since she got to enjoy the very fine sight of Graham's toned backside as he leaned.

"Did you have a good time?" Emma asked.

Adelaide jumped at her friend's voice. She forced a smile and turned away from their companions with great difficulty. "Yes, I did. I'm so glad you invited me—it was a welcome respite from the boredom and discomfort of my usual supper company."

Emma smiled. "And you weren't put off by Graham being here? I had no idea James was even going to see him today, let alone would invite him to supper."

"Of course not," Adelaide said, and meant it. "He was a charming companion."

Emma expression softened with relief. "That's funny, for he described you the same way earlier. But he *was*, wasn't he? I never knew him before his engagement to Meg, and everything happened so quickly after I married James that I've spent little time with him. But tonight he was the man my husband has always described as his best and truest friend."

Adelaide allowed herself another glance at Graham. He was leaning on his cue now, and to her surprise he was staring straight at her. He smiled as he was caught and shocked her by winking.

She spun back toward Emma, her breath suddenly short. What was he doing? Not a week before he'd been pinning Lydia Ford to a table and kissing her until she was weak in the knees. Tonight he was flirting with a wallflower and acting like it was all bloody normal.

And he said *she* was the most frustrating person on earth. Except when she looked at him, she didn't feel frustrated. She felt...well, she felt things she wasn't meant to feel as Lady Adelaide, spinster daughter of a dead earl. As Lydia, perhaps she could feel them. Pursue them even.

"What do you think of him?" Emma asked.

Adelaide jerked her face to Emma. Was she playing matchmaker? But her friend's expression was calm and unreadable. Of course she wouldn't. Woman like Adelaide didn't belong with men like Graham.

She dropped her gaze and sighed. "Well, I hardly know him well enough to formulate an opinion one way or another," she said. "Now, you mentioned something at supper about a ladies society for charitable works. I'd be very interested in that."

Emma hesitated, and Adelaide could see her attempts at changing the subject were a bit heavy-handed, but Emma allowed for it. She began to talk about the group and Adelaide forced herself to truly attend.

But in the back of her mind she heard a voice whispering to her. Her own voice that told her she certainly had an opinion about Graham, even if she wouldn't dare share it with Emma.

She *liked* him. And that was too dangerous not to acknowledge. She would have to tread carefully now.

It was the only way to protect herself.

CHAPTER SEVEN

The applause was still booming in the theatre as Adelaide stepped into her dressing room. Normally she reveled in the accolades, but tonight they felt a little dull. She was distracted and she'd felt that in her performance. In the second act she'd missed a line entirely and her co-star, Robin, had smirked with pleasure and said something snide about it as they rushed to change costumes for their final scene.

"Wretched man," she muttered as she took in a deep breath she wished would calm her and moved toward her dressing table.

It was then she heard a sniffle from the corner of the room, a tiny area behind her costumes. She pivoted toward it.

"Who's there?" she called out as she pushed the dresses away and revealed Melinda sitting beneath, tears streaking her cheeks.

"Gracious, Melinda!" Adelaide gasped, leaning down to grasp her friend's arms and pull her to her feet. "What is it?"

Melinda was trembling as Adelaide guided her to the settee and they sat together.

"It—it's that *horrid* Sir Archibald," Melinda admitted when she had stopped crying and could catch her breath. "Oh, Lydia, he came backstage during the performance again."

Adelaide clenched her teeth. That man was a menace. "Toby didn't stop him?"

Melinda shook her head. "He was busy with the show, of course. I was standing in the wings, saying your lines along with you and suddenly he was right behind me."

Adelaide studied her. Melinda was often a bit silly and she was prone to theatrics that went beyond the stage, but in this moment Adelaide could tell she was truly upset.

"What did Sir Archibald do?" she whispered.

Melinda shivered. "He yanked me into the corner behind the stage, the darkest one. He pinned me against the wall and kissed me." She gagged. "He tasted of sweat and cheap cigars and whiskey. Then he started grinding his hard, disgusting cock on me."

Adelaide grasped both her hands. "Oh, dearest, he didn't…"

She trailed off and Melinda turned her face. "No. I managed to push free of him and ran. That's why I hid in the dressing room. He was looking for me, I could hear him blustering up the hall, calling me all matter of names, but he didn't find me."

Lydia let out a sigh of relief. "I'm so sorry he hurt you," she said. "But I'm glad it wasn't worse. We really must tell Toby to find someone to guard the back. There are too many men of Sir Archibald's ilk who think they can take what isn't offered to them, especially by women such as us."

"*Please* don't say anything to Toby," Melinda whispered, her cheeks flaring.

Adelaide stared at her. "Why ever not? It is his job as manager to ensure—"

"I know, and he'd feel awful if he knew the truth." Melinda ducked her head. "Anyway, Toby did hire some men, but Sir Archibald actually crowed about paying them off."

Rage pulsed through Adelaide at the thought. There were so many men from her sphere who thought they were entitled to more than a woman was willing to give. Their power was a weapon and a shield. "But certainly we *must* protect you and the others."

Melinda shrugged. "The next time I'll be sure Robin's

understudy stands with me. Or I'll stand near Toby. That should help, shouldn't it?"

Adelaide wasn't so certain, but before she could say more about it there was a knock on her door and Toby, himself, ducked in.

He shot a glance at Melinda and the smile on his face fell. "What is it, Melly?"

Melinda brightened, putting on her best stage face. "Nothing at all, Toby. We were just practicing a few lines together." She leaned in. "What's that you're hiding behind the door?"

Toby didn't seem convinced by Melinda's lie, but he shifted a vase of beautiful flowers into view. "Flowers for Lydia," he declared. "From—"

"Me," a voice finished for him, and the door was pushed open all the way to reveal Graham standing there.

Adelaide rushed to her feet as she stared at him. She'd been thinking of nothing else but him since the previous night with James and Emma. He was the cause of her distraction both then and now.

"Your Grace," she managed to croak out as she watched him enter the room. Fill the room. Steal the air. He was impossible. But once again, he seemed not to recognize her for who she truly was as he smiled down at her.

"*Mrs.* Ford," he said, just as formal but with a lilt of teasing to his tone.

Melinda had shoved to her feet as he came in and now she hustled to the door. "Come, Toby, I'll help you with the break down."

Adelaide didn't take her eyes off Graham as the two exited, closing the door behind them as they did. She swallowed hard. Alone again. She'd been alone with this man more in the past few days than she had been with any man since…

Well, since a good long time ago.

"Was your friend quite well?" he asked.

She stared at the unexpected question. "Melinda?"

He nodded. "She looked as though she had been crying."

Of course he would notice. Adelaide was beginning to realize that while Graham put on a face of distance, he was actually very aware of his surroundings and those within them.

"She's…fine," Adelaide said, since there was no use in telling him the truth about Sir Archibald. What would he do about it? Men of his rank were allowed to do what they liked. She and Melinda would have to work out their own way to handle this.

He tilted his head, as if reading that response, but then he moved closer. "You were wonderful tonight."

"I was distracted," she admitted before she thought it through.

He arched a brow. "By what?"

He was so close now. Too close. He was looming, though there was nothing intimidating about it. Just alluring. Warm. Strong. Safe.

Although the last thing Graham was was *safe*. She had no idea why that descriptor had come to mind. Nor why she couldn't think of any response to his question except for the truth.

"You," she finally whispered.

His eyes went wide and then a broad grin spread across his face. It was feral and possessive and hot and so damned real that she fought not to launch herself into his arms. That end seemed inevitable, but she was going to lean away from it as long as she could.

"You were distracted by me?" he practically purred. "You flatter, Lydia."

"It isn't meant as a compliment, Graham," she retorted, then clapped a hand to her lips. He had told *Adelaide* to call him Graham, not Lydia. "I-I'm sorry, my lord—Y-Your Grace," she stammered. "That was spoken out of turn."

His smile hadn't faded. "I like that you call me by my given name," he drawled. "I would much rather be that which you moaned than my title, which was last held by a bastard whose very memory turns my stomach."

Adelaide hesitated at that unexpected confession, a brief glimpse into a past she found she desperately wanted to know. He didn't give her the chance, though, for he continued talking. "I came here because I can't stop thinking of you either, Lydia. You are all that has been in my head since the last time I touched you."

Adelaide frowned, unexpected jealousy ripping through her. Jealousy of herself, which was ridiculous and incredibly confusing. But he was saying that while he danced with her-*Adelaide* her, while he talked to her, while he teased her and winked at her and generally made her feel...*nervous*, he'd been thinking of Lydia Ford.

Who wasn't even real.

Except right now she *felt* very real, especially when Graham was reaching out a hand and sliding his fingers along her jawline. His touch was electric, and she shivered at the power of her body's immediate response. She felt hot and cold at the same time, her nipples tingled and her sex felt heavy and full and wet. There was no controlling that. In truth, she didn't want to control it, because it had been a very long time since she felt such a need, and never before had it been so earnest and powerful.

He leaned in and she didn't pull away. She just lifted her mouth to his and let him kiss her.

Unlike the first time he'd claimed her mouth, this time he didn't sweep her away. He didn't back her into a table. He didn't grind against her like they were animals in undeniable heat. This time he kissed her gently, his tongue probing her lips and then her mouth when she opened on a sigh.

When he pulled back, his pupils were dilated until there was only a sliver of blue remaining, and his breath was short. "Lydia, come home with me."

Her eyes went wide. There was no mistaking him. He wasn't asking her to his home for tea. If she took his offer, he would make love to her. And every rational part of her screamed at the dangers of that. The dangers of entering an affair with a powerful man, the dangers of him discovering her true identity, and the dangers of involving more than her quaking body once she had surrendered to this man who already set her entirely on her head, whether she was Lydia or Adelaide.

And yet her rational voice was so easily quieted when he glided his hand down the slope of her neck, pushing aside her hair and tracing her collarbone with gentle strokes of his fingertips.

"Please, Lydia."

She swallowed. Despite her wicked foray into the theatre, her life was truly set in stone. She was a spinster who lived with a guardian who despised her, and had no prospects for a future. Not ever again would she be offered this kind of passion.

And she wanted it. She wanted him.

"Very well," she choked out. "Yes. But I—I'll take my own carriage."

He seemed surprised both by her acquiescence and her caveat, but he didn't argue. He only nodded as he slipped her hand into the crook of his elbow and led her from the relative safety of the dressing room and toward the wild and unpredictable abandon of what would happen next.

Graham had arrived home first and waved off his servants, telling them to go to bed. He didn't want politeness and pretending tonight. He just wanted Lydia.

Now he paced in his foyer, glancing occasionally through the window as he waited for her carriage to arrive. The small, unmarked one she hadn't allowed him to help her into. She'd just asked him to tell her driver the directions, then slammed the door in his face.

He didn't know how to read the woman. Perhaps that was part of the draw. She was alive and unpredictable and nothing like anyone he'd ever known. He needed that after the past few months. Hell, after the past few years. He needed it more than he needed spinsters who challenged him, certainly.

He stopped his pacing at that thought. Where had it come from? Images of Adelaide, in a moment like this, just as he was about to bed a woman who was her polar opposite? It was unseemly.

Well, perhaps not her *polar* opposite. They both had blonde hair, not that he could really tell the true color of Adelaide's thanks to her relentlessly stern chignon. And their eyes were blue. But Lydia's were wide and sensual, where Adelaide's were hidden beneath those spectacles she never removed.

"Why are you comparing them?" he growled out loud, jolting himself back in line. "Ridiculous."

Lydia's carriage turned into his drive, and he straightened as he moved to the door. He opened it to watch her driver help her down. She looked up at his townhouse and he awaited her reaction. It was magnificent. Every woman said so. He hated the place, but that was another story entirely.

But Lydia simply pursed her lips, seemingly unaffected by the huge building, and her eyes lowered to settle on him. In that unguarded moment, lit only by the lights in the house behind him, she looked...afraid. Uncertain. His stomach clenched at that sight, for it was almost innocent.

But she couldn't be innocent, could she? Most ladies of the stage weren't. And she was *Mrs.* Ford. He still wasn't sure if that was a lie or the truth.

The look flitted away as she moved up the stairs toward him, and his brain emptied of all questions and thoughts and all feelings except for that renewed drive to claim this woman in the most primal way he could muster. His cock ached as she stopped before him and stared up into his face.

"Are you going to invite me in?" she asked.

He blinked, realizing he'd been standing mute for almost thirty seconds. "Of course, please."

He stepped aside and she entered the house. Once again, she only gave it a cursory look over and then she turned toward him, her hands folded in front of herself.

"Don't most men of your stature have servants, Your Grace?" she asked, a lilt of teasing to her tone.

He shut the door and leaned back against it, staring at her. Great Christ, but she was magnificent. Her hair was still down in wild waves around her shoulders and her small but perfectly formed breasts. He wanted to see her with only that hair covering her.

"I sent them to bed," he said. "I didn't want to be disturbed."

She smiled slightly. "A good idea," she whispered.

He couldn't hold back anymore. With a low groan, he moved to her and cupped the back of her head, dropping his mouth against hers with what he knew was out of control animal heat. She didn't resist him, but reached up to clutch his lapels, arching against him with none of the innocence he'd sensed in her on the drive.

He tasted her, like honey and sherry and something that was just her, just perfect. And he wanted that scent and that taste to be dumped over him, he wanted to bathe in it. Be burned with it. Something to make it never go away.

He pulled back, panting, and motioned to the stairway. "Shall we?"

She nodded and reached out a hand. He stared at her slender fingers, ungloved as they touched his. She folded her hand around his, and for a moment he was flooded with a sense of incredible peace. He forgot everything that normally haunted him and took a deep breath.

But need was still need, drive was still drive, and he moved up the stairs at last, drawing her up to his room and shaking with the power of everything he wanted to do to her. Now he could, and he wasn't about to waste a moment she had granted him.

CHAPTER EIGHT

Adelaide could hardly breathe as Graham drew her into a chamber at the end of the long hallway. She hadn't given a damn about the rest of his house—she'd been in many a fine manor in her life—but in this room she took in every detail.

It was a large bedroom, with a roaring fire along one wall and large, four-poster bed opposite. The colors were masculine blues and steely grays, and they fit the man who now stood behind her, watching her as she looked over the room they would share for what she hoped would be a few hours.

There was danger in that, of course, but she'd manage it. She always did.

"Look at me," he whispered.

His tone was so rough, so low and pulsing with desire that she couldn't deny him. She slowly pivoted and faced him, sucking in a breath as she did. He was still perfectly done up, not a hair out of place or a piece of clothing wrinkled. And yet he looked undone, wicked, fallen. And she wanted to strip him down and give herself over in every wanton way she'd ever let herself imagine.

"You've done this before, I assume," he said softly.

She tilted her head at the question, even as it struck terror in her heart. Why would he ask after her innocence? If she were Adelaide standing here, she could understand it. There was an act she performed in her daily life that would lead him to believe she hadn't made love before. But as Lydia, he should have assumed she was not untouched.

"I have," she said, keeping her tone cool and light. "I assume *you* have."

His mouth quirked up in one of those rare and spectacular grins. "Oh yes," he said, reaching out to catch the sash on her simple gown and draw her close. "Though I do admit it's been a while."

She shivered as he drew her up against him, her curves molding easily against his hardness and her body reacted accordingly. She was melting, burning, being assimilated by his desire. She might not survive it. And she didn't care.

"I hope…" she whispered as she reached a hand up to touch his chest. He hissed in a breath as she did so, and that gave her confidence. "That this will be worth the wait."

He growled rather than answer and spun her around so their positions were reversed. The door now pressed to her back and he loomed up over her, caging her in with strong, powerful arms as he stared down into her face.

They were too close, and she tensed again, terrified he would recognize something of Adelaide in her Lydia façade. But he didn't. He merely leaned in and began to kiss the column of her neck. Of course he wouldn't see Adelaide. He didn't think of her. Not like this.

She pushed aside her disappointment at that stark fact and focused on the way his mouth moved against her. He was firm, sucking her flesh, but gentle enough that it didn't hurt. She clenched her fists against his chest, shifting as pure desire flowed through her already ultra-sensitive body.

She loosened the button on his jacket and slid her hands beneath, and he hissed out a sound of pleasure that was all but lost against her skin. The wavering control of it spurred her on, though, and she pushed the coat to the floor. His waistcoat came next and she wrestled it open and tossed it aside just as easily.

She stopped then. She had to. He pulled away so she couldn't do more. But he didn't do it to stop her. He did it so that he could turn her, pressing her hands to the smooth, cool surface of the door with one hand and unbuttoning her dress with the other. She arched as the fabric parted, sending cooler air against her skin. She wore nothing beneath, after all, for her costume at the theatre didn't allow for undergarments.

When he pushed the dress lower and discovered that for himself, he let out a low groan and then his lips were on her skin. He pushed her hair aside and dragged his mouth along the back of her neck, lower to trace her spine until her gown got in the way again.

Only then did he tug it down and let it pool at her feet, leaving her only in her plain slippers and equally plain stockings.

"Turn around," he whispered, his voice a plea and an order and a prayer all at once.

She clenched her fists before she did it, screwing up her courage as best she could. Her experiences in the past, the ones she tried very hard not to think of, had not included a man looking at her utterly naked. And now it would be this man who did.

This man.

She turned and found he had stepped back. He stared at her, his eyes feasting from the top of her head to the tips of her toes. She had no idea how he felt about what he saw, and she brought a shaking hand in front of her sex as she turned her face to escape his heavy scrutiny.

"Lydia," he whispered, that false name now piercing her like a sword because every time he said it, for it reminded her what he really wanted.

She pushed those reactions away and said, "Yes?"

He folded his fingers around her wrist and gently pushed her hand away. "You don't have to hide from me," he assured her.

She forced herself to look up and found a gentle expression on his otherwise hard face. A strange dichotomy that she was drawn to, just as she was drawn to everything about this man.

"I'm at a disadvantage," she managed to grind out, her

voice roughened by desire and fear. "For I am undone and you are perfectly...*perfect*."

"Far from that," he reassured her with a low chuckle. "But I think you mean I'm clothed. Which is something I intend to remedy right now."

He untied his cravat as he said the words, unwinding it in a few motions, then dropping it at his side. As he lifted his hands to unfasten his shirt, she found herself leaning forward. His body had been a fascination to her from the first moment he touched her, pinned her so mercilessly against that table. And as he parted his shirt and pulled it away from his body, she stopped breathing.

He was as hard as he felt when she was in his arms. All muscle and sinew, from his broad shoulders to his uncommonly perfect arms to the faint ripples in his stomach. He had a small scar on his ribcage and another up on his shoulder, but those things only made him more attractive, not less.

"Your eyes are wide as saucers," he said, his tone laced with both humor and concern. "Are you *certain* you've done this before, Lydia?"

She swallowed. "Not with anyone like you."

"What is someone like me?" he asked, but his hands dropped to the placard of his trousers and he slowly unfastened it, never taking his eyes from her.

"I hardly know how to describe you, for I only repeat the words others write and am no poet," she murmured, her throat thick, her body trembling. "The Bard would compare you to a summer's day."

"That was written for a woman, wasn't it?" he said with a shake of his head.

"I don't care, it fits," she choked as he lowered the placard and revealed the thick, heavy, hard thrust of his cock. "You are golden and not just because of the color of your hair. You are spectacular. And I am fully aware that this is fleeting and so I should enjoy it, much as one does a perfect summer day."

His smile faltered at her last sentence, but she gave him no space in which to reply or argue. She stepped up to him, bolder than she felt, and wound her arms around his neck to kiss him. She felt him shuffle, kicking aside his trousers, and then he cupped her naked backside suddenly and drew her fully against him.

Her world all but shattered. There was nothing left except her soft body against his hard one, his arms cradling her so safe and tight and warm, his cock nudging her belly, so unsafe and so wanted.

He turned her once more, backing her toward his bed, and her legs began to shake as he lifted her on the edge. This was going to happen. It *was* happening. And she'd never wanted something more in her entire life.

He maneuvered her onto the pillows without breaking his seeking mouth from hers and she settled back into the softness as she glided her fingers into his thick blond hair and pulled it out of the queue that bound the locks.

He pulled back to look down at her and she couldn't breathe. With his hair down he was the fallen angel he pretended not to be. Sinful and sensual and leading her into temptation from which she would not escape unchanged.

He grinned down at her, infinitely wicked, and then he lowered his mouth not to her lips, but to her chest. He traced her collarbone with his tongue and she gasped at the flood of unexpected sensation that raced through her. He dragged his lips lower, cresting over one breast before he latched firmly onto her nipple.

She drove her fingers into his hair once more, calling out his name in a strangled cry that seemed to shatter the silence of the room. He suckled harder, swirling his tongue around and around and around until she was dizzy with pleasure. Then he drew his mouth to her other breast and did the same, arousing her to a point where she feared she might combust.

But he didn't take her. Not yet. His mouth moved lower, over her flat stomach, licking her hip, her thigh, and then he spread her legs wide and stopped.

She struggled to sit up, staring at him as he positioned himself between her legs. "What are you doing?" she gasped out.

His brow wrinkled as he looked up at her. "No one has done this for you?"

She shook her head slowly. She wasn't even certain what *this* was.

He frowned. "Lydia, if you are untouched, I need you to be honest with me now. I don't want to hurt you, and I will if you have never been with a man."

She stared at him. Here he was, with a woman she had created, who most men of his stature would see as only just above a whore. And yet he was gentle with her. Tender, even. He didn't want to hurt her.

"My experiences are limited," she admitted. "One man, three years ago. He didn't do any of the things you've done to me tonight. But he did take me. I'm not a virgin, Graham. And I don't want you to stop, so please, please don't."

He tilted his head, almost as if he recognized that there was honesty here amongst all her other lies. There was, after all. The story Adelaide had just told was her own, not Lydia Ford's.

"I'm not going to stop," he promised. "And I'm going to make up for whatever bad experience you had in the past."

As he said the words, he ducked his head and suddenly his tongue was on her, in her. She let out a shocked and gasping cry and lifted her hips. What was this? This powerful feeling that pulsed through her entire being as he licked her ceaselessly. She had touched herself in the past, of course. She knew about the release of orgasm. But this was something far more powerful than anything she'd ever done for herself.

This was magical.

He sucked her clitoris and she jolted as an electric current of pleasure seemed to lift her from the bed against her will. He smiled against her wet body and placed a hand on her stomach, holding her steady as he focused all his attention, all his passion, all his talent on that hooded bundle of nerves.

She ground against him, whimpering and murmuring along

the building path of pleasure. And then, suddenly, she reached the edge of the cliff and she fell. Her hips jolted, unable to be tamed even by his strong hand. She let out a keening cry, clenching at the coverlet, tugging at his hair, digging her heels into his bed as wave after powerful wave of explosive sensation hit her. He continued to lick her through it all, dragging the moment out until she was trembling against the pillows, spent and weak with what she'd just experienced.

Only then did he crawl back up the length of her body. Only then did he kiss her and let her taste the flavor of her release. She clung to him, desperate as she returned that kiss and felt the ache of wanting him still pulsing low between her legs.

He positioned himself as they kissed, opening her wider, pushing his cock against her entrance. And then he was sliding inside.

Her previous experience had been a blessedly brief exploration of pain followed by humiliation and heartbreak. This was not that. Her body stretched, accommodating him like she was meant to do so, despite his size. And it felt *good*, which she had never expected.

He lifted his head, watching her carefully as he withdrew and returned in one skillful stroke. She dug her fingers into his shoulders, lifting to meet him as her world condensed down into this one act, this one place, this one man.

He began to take her, slowly at first, swiveling his hips, as certain at this act as he seemed to be in all else. But as her gasps and cries increased, as the pleasure that had receded after his skillful mouth returned with full force, she could see the edges of his control fray.

His neck tightened, the veins outlined against the flesh, and he grunted in pleasure, part man, part beast, everything she wanted.

Her world began to shatter for a second time as he ground against her, and his thrusts increased as she mewled and rubbed to find even more pleasure. She saw the strain as he tried to wait, tried to draw out her experience as long as possible. Then at last he shouted, "Lydia!" and pulled away from her, his seed splashing against her stomach as he spent.

She caught his shoulders, drawing him down against her, pressing her mouth to his in wonder and gratitude as she wished, hoped and prayed that this stunning moment could last forever. And knew it would be over far too soon.

Lydia lay across Graham's chest, her hand gently clenching and unclenching against his skin and her hair tickling his arms. It had been twenty minutes since they'd made love. Normally by now he would be exiting the bed of his lover, making some excuse to send her away or to go himself.

Of course, the last time he'd taken a lover had been years ago. His engagement to Meg had made such things awkward and he hadn't exactly wanted *anyone* near him in the months since their affiliation ended so badly.

But tonight he felt no desire to run, nor to send Lydia away. Tonight holding her felt…right. And that was slightly terrifying.

She lifted her head, almost as if she read his mind and smiled at him. "I should go."

The comfort he'd been feeling fled with those three small words, and he examined her face to see what her motives were. He couldn't tell. She was too good of an actress to let him see anything she didn't want him to see.

"Back to *Mr.* Ford?" he asked, thinking of the story she'd told of one lover long ago. He believed that to be true, but she was a good actress. It might not be.

She arched a brow and leaned up on her elbow, tracing a light pattern on his chest. "I think you know full well that pretending to be married is one way women in the theatre protect themselves."

When she said *protect*, his stomach clenched and his mind took him back to terrible images of screaming and thudding and death and loss. He only just reined in his anxiety at that and said, "Have you ever been threatened?"

She caught her breath, and he knew the answer. But she shook her head, lied. "Not as much as others," she said at last.

His lips pursed. To be honest, he'd never put much thought into women of the theatre or the night or the servant quarters. His world felt so far removed from theirs until now. But he could see how what all of them did put them at risk. What could they do to put off men with more power? Men who didn't accept no as an answer if they wanted something badly enough?

Hell, even women in his circle had very little recourse if they were threatened or harmed. He knew that from bitter experience.

"What you do is dangerous," he said.

"Sometimes," she conceded, trouble in her stare. Then it flickered away and was replaced by something else. Something hotter. Something knowing. She lifted up and brushed her lips to his with an easy sensuality that ground his thoughts to a halt almost instantly. "But dangerous isn't always bad," she whispered.

She pulled away and he let her go, for as much as he wanted her, she had set afire a flame in his mind. One that was far from pleasant. He watched her step into her gown, watched her get ready to leave him, and he sat up slowly.

"Lydia, I would not want to see you...hurt," he said.

She paused with her back toward him, and there was tension in her body language that he didn't understand. Was she upset at his confession? Was she fearful of consequences she would face, ones she didn't want to share with him?

She looked at him at last and she had a smile so false that he almost flinched away from it. She leaned in and kissed him once more. "It isn't your responsibility, Your Grace," she said softly. "Good night."

She left then, without so much as a backward glance. He did nothing to stop her, partly because he realized he couldn't. Partly because he wasn't exactly certain what he would do if he did. What would he say? She was not asking for help. He wasn't even certain she needed it. And yet he was left with an uneasiness in his chest.

Like he'd just missed an opportunity that might never come again.

CHAPTER NINE

"Did you know that I heard a racket last night?"

Adelaide jerked her head up from the pretty pair of gloves she had been eyeing on the table in the dressmaker's shop and stared at her aunt. Opal was worrying a necklace around her neck, her gaze wide and troubled.

"A racket?" she asked, and tried to sound nonchalant.

The racket, of course, had been her sneaking back into her aunt's home after her wild and wonderful night with Graham. Normally her maid, one of the few people who knew the truth about her, greeted her at a set time after her shows. But since she had returned so late the girl had been forced to sit in the kitchen and had fallen asleep as she waited. When Adelaide had knocked, poor Rebecca had awoken with a start and toppled over a broom. The two had been forced to scurry away before they were caught.

"Yes, a crash in the kitchen after two in the morning," Opal said. "I thought it was an intruder and I rang for Smith."

"You woke Smith up?" Adelaide said, feeling very guilty for that fact. The kindly butler was already so put upon with Opal's odd moods and occasional outbursts, she hated to think she'd caused him more grief.

"Of course I did. What was I to do, go down myself and be..." Opal dropped her voice so the shopkeep wouldn't hear her. "...*accosted* in my kitchen?"

"No, Smith is better suited for that, isn't he?" Adelaide muttered, and her aunt glared.

"It is what I pay him for, isn't it?" Opal snapped.

Technically that was true, so Adelaide shrugged. She wasn't in the mood to argue with her aunt at any rate. Digging deeper might only lead to trouble. "I assume he found nothing?"

Opal sighed, almost as if she were disappointed they hadn't all been murdered in their beds by robbers. "No. A fallen broom, he thought, perhaps turned over by a mouse."

"Then there is nothing to fear, is there?" Adelaide said with a false smile as relief washed over her. Once again she had somehow escaped detection. "The mystery is solved and all is well."

Her aunt looked less than convinced, but before she could continue the conversation, a voice called out from across the shop. "Lady Adelaide!"

Adelaide turned toward it, but any happiness she had at being interrupted dissolved when she saw the owner of the voice that said her name. The Duchess of Crestwood was coming across the shop, her smile wide and her eyes locked on Adelaide.

Adelaide found herself shifting as the woman reached her, setting her shoulders back, widening her stance a little. Like they were going to battle. Ridiculous.

"Your Grace," she said as calmly as she could. "How unexpected."

The duchess tilted her head slightly and then turned her attention toward Adelaide's chaperone. "Good afternoon. Lady Opal, isn't it? What a lovely name."

Opal actually looked impressed as she looked the duchess up and down, not that Adelaide could blame her. The woman exuded such confidence and grace, and it was well-known how much she was liked and respected in Society. Her marriage to Crestwood had changed that somewhat—people whispered, of course, but if anyone could overcome that, it would be this woman.

Graham was another story, though, and that made Adelaide

push away any unexpected respect she felt for the duchess and harden herself.

"Lady Opal?" the shopkeeper said, motioning to the fabric her aunt had demanded he fetch from the back.

"Excuse me, won't you?" Opal said, and Adelaide's heart sank. Normally she did not mourn when her aunt walked away, but today she wanted to race after her.

Instead she turned back to find the duchess watching her, an appraising look on her face. "I'm so happy to see you again."

Adelaide cleared her throat, uncertain how to proceed. "Thank you, Your Grace. Though I don't know why."

"Meg, truly you must call me Meg," the duchess said. "And I'm pleased because I know you are a great friend of Emma's and I adore her almost beyond reason. So we *must* be friends, mustn't we?"

Adelaide shifted slightly. She recognized the dark feeling that bloomed in her chest as she looked at the duchess...*Meg*. Jealousy. Jealousy of her fast friendship with Emma, who had once been closest to Adelaide. And jealousy of whatever this woman had once shared with Graham. Even knowing how it had ended, even knowing he hadn't loved her, she couldn't help but wonder if he'd ever kissed her. Touched her.

Being that they'd been engaged for so long, she had to believe *something* had passed between them. How could anyone be with Graham and not want to feel his arms wrapped around them?

Apparently she had been considering those thoughts for too long, for Meg smiled slightly. "Well, *I* would like to be friends, at any rate."

Adelaide gasped. "Oh, yes. Of course. I'm certain we will see each other from time to time given our relationships to Emma."

Meg's forehead wrinkled slightly. "I hope that will be true. And perhaps one day we will also see more of Northfield back in our circle as well."

Adelaide stared at her. "I'm afraid I wouldn't know

anything about that," she said, her tone far cooler as her hackles raised. How dare this woman act like Graham could simply slip back into the way things were after what had happened to him? She felt a strong desire to defend him yet again. And it *still* wasn't her place.

Even after what they'd shared last night.

"Don't you?" Meg said. "Emma had said something about you two developing a bit of a friendship of sorts."

Adelaide froze, her mind dragging her to images of Graham's mouth between her legs, of him rising over her as he took her, of his searing kiss that made her whole body so damned weak.

She shook those thoughts aside. "I hardly know the man, so I don't know why Emma would say that."

"He's a good friend to have," Meg insisted, her tone suddenly growing faraway. "Steadfast and loyal."

Adelaide couldn't help it. She folded her arms firmly across her chest. "Seems he has not always received that from his friends in return."

Meg flinched, and Adelaide immediately wished she could take the harsh words back. After all, Meg was Emma's sister-in-law. If she weren't more prudent, she could end up losing Emma, and for what? A man who probably didn't think of her at all? *Lydia* was what he wanted. A fantasy that didn't truly exist. A woman who would disappear eventually, for there was no way she could keep up her double life indefinitely.

Meg looked off toward the door, tears in her eyes. "The situation between Simon and Graham and me was…complicated," she said softly.

Adelaide caught her breath. "I really don't think you should tell me—"

"Normally I wouldn't speak of it, but I saw you with him at the party a few days ago," Meg interrupted. "There was something between you. I may not have loved Graham, he certainly didn't love me. But I knew him. Once upon a time, I knew him. If you are a friend to him, as Emma claims and you deny, then I think he needs one. And clearly you wish to defend him and I think he needs that, too."

Adelaide shifted, for what she felt for Graham was really very complicated. Desire, yes. Frustration, yes. Jealousy…yes. And she didn't want to face any of that yet. Or ever. And yet she *did* want to know more. She wanted to know what Graham wouldn't say.

"Wh-why did it happen as it did?" she asked.

Meg stared at her for what felt like an eternity, until Adelaide shifted with discomfort. Until she began to search for a way to change the subject.

"I don't normally speak of it," Meg whispered at last. "But I loved Simon from the first moment I met him."

"Then why did you agree to marry Northfield?" Adelaide asked.

"I didn't." Meg ducked her head. "James arranged it. We were all so young when it happened, none of us had the capacity to figure out how to abandon the plan. None of us had the courage to take the first step. That nearly cost me the love of my life. And it has cost Simon one of the truest friends he's ever had. Seeing his pain and knowing the depth of Graham's is the only mar upon my happiness."

Adelaide bit her lip. Here she had seen Meg and Simon as the evildoers in the situation, but she could see how truly bothered Meg was by her husband's pain. More than that, she could see how much she was hurt by Graham's.

"Is there any way to—to *fix* it?" Adelaide asked.

"What you must understand," Meg said softly, "is that James, Simon, Graham and all the others are like brothers. *Were* like brothers. My greatest wish is that they can overcome this and Graham will return to us. Home where he belongs. How that happens, well, I suppose we'll all see."

There was something about the way Meg speared her with a stare that made Adelaide's heart jump. That made her feel that Meg thought she would have some role in Graham's reunion with his friends. But that placed far too much importance on her.

More than he would ever give.

She turned her face. "My aunt appears to be finished with her transaction, so I must excuse myself," she said.

Meg nodded. "Of course. It was nice to see you again, Adelaide." She leaned in. "And I do hope that someday you will come to like me and we can be friends."

Meg squeezed her arm gently, and then she turned to walk to the shopkeeper. "Mr. Evans, how wonderful to see you again!"

But as Opal came back, Adelaide couldn't help but stare at Meg. The directness she had just encountered wasn't something she was accustomed to. Nor were the feelings that directness had inspired, feelings toward the duchess, but also toward Graham.

Graham thundered through the park on his horse, urging the mount to go faster as he sped along the lanes, ignoring the glares of the other park-goers. His mind was spinning too quickly not to move his body just as fast.

Almost like he was going to outrun something. Only he couldn't.

He had made love to Lydia Ford less than twenty-four hours before. And it had been spectacular, and yet he couldn't help but feel…troubled. Incomplete, no matter how satisfying he'd found the experience.

He didn't like it. He liked when things were neat and careful and well planned.

"Exactly why your life is such a tangle right now," he grunted to himself, slowing Samson as he steered the animal onto one of the forested paths that went farther into the wooded parts of the park. Alongside the riders, walkers strolled. Ladies with parasols, gentlemen with canes. They were all there to see and to be seen.

Graham felt very exposed as he rode through them,

knowing their eyes turned on him. Knowing their whispers addressed the scandal he couldn't escape. Except, it seemed, when he was with Lydia.

He glanced up the road and his eyes fell on the form of a lady standing on the grass with her maid. For a moment, his heart leapt, for he thought certain it was Lydia herself. But then the lady turned and he jolted again as he recognized the too-tight chignon, the spectacles perched on a fine nose.

"Great God!" he called out as he slowed his horse to a stop and swung down. "Lady Adelaide."

She gasped as he stepped toward her and then glanced over her shoulder into the grassy area. Her maid met her eyes and then she smiled as she stepped away a step or two. Close enough to call them chaperoned, far enough that they could talk.

"Your Grace," Adelaide said, her tone a bit breathless. "I-I did not expect to see you here."

"I haven't ridden in the park for some time," he admitted. "Too many eyes, rather like a ball. But I needed air today. I needed to think."

She turned her face away slightly. "I see."

"What brings you out?" he asked. "You aren't alone, are you?"

Her lips pursed slightly and a look of resignation crossed her face. He found he didn't like the change. It made him want to...*fix* whatever was bothering her somehow.

A ridiculous notion.

Adelaide glanced over her shoulder again. "My aunt likes to take a walk in the park each day at this time. Often she insists I join her, though she finds any excuse to walk off from me."

Graham followed her line of vision and saw a rather severe-looking woman standing in a group of other ladies, talking. Her blonde hair was streaked with gray and she was almost rail-thin. Despite that, he could see a bit of Adelaide in her, though he far preferred his companion to her aunt.

"How long have you lived with her?" he asked, finding himself truly interested in the answer, not just making small talk.

Adelaide sucked in a breath, almost imperceptible except that he was so entirely focused on her in that moment. Then she said, "My parents died when I was ten. I've lived with my aunt ever since."

There was a pain in her voice that was so palpable that it stung him. It sounded like his own pain when it came to those he'd lost.

"How?" he asked softly. "If you don't mind sharing."

She stared up at him for what felt like a lifetime, and he could see she was trying to decide if she should tell him. If she trusted him. If he was playing a game with her, as she had accused him of the night he'd danced with her at the ball.

"A fever," she said at last. "He first, she a few days later."

"I'm sorry," he said, and meant it with all his heart. "Losing one parent is hard enough. To lose two that you loved…" He trailed off, and now she looked at him more closely. Like she could see he was a kindred spirit in loss. Which, of course, he was. He could also see her desire to press him more on the subject. His body clenched and he turned away. "Fine weather we're having."

She hesitated and then nodded. "Indeed. I've never seen an autumn so fine. I suppose it is why all the peacocks are out on display. Soon the rain and cold will force them back indoors where they can only preen in time to music."

He laughed at her dry judgment. "You have a fine view on those of our class."

She shrugged. "When one observes from afar, I suppose one cannot help but judge. Perhaps I'm too harsh."

"No, I think you're spot on. We're all trained to display, as you say." He shook his head. "It does get tiresome. To always be…*performing*."

She caught her breath a second time, and when he looked at her, her eyes were wide beneath her spectacles and her hands trembled ever so slightly at her sides. He might have asked her about it, for the reaction took him aback, but before he could, she glanced over her shoulder once more.

"Oh, bollocks, here she comes," she muttered.

His eyes went wide at her unexpected curse, and he looked at her aunt was coming toward them. The woman did look *angry* to see her niece talking to him.

"Is she so very bad as that?" he whispered. "I would think she'd like to see you talking with a duke."

Adelaide shot him a glare. "Quite full of ourselves, aren't we?"

He smiled in the hopes it would calm her a little. "Always, my dear. Dear God, she does look cross."

Adelaide nodded. "She does." She could say no more, though, for the lady had reached them at last. "Aunt Opal, I do hope your talk with your friends was pleasant. Are you acquainted with the Duke of Northfield?"

"Your Grace," Lady Opal said with a chill to her tone that could have frozen a man's ballocks in a heartbeat.

Graham bowed his head. "My lady. I was passing through the park and saw Lady Adelaide standing by the path. I wanted to say hello."

"And so you have," Lady Opal said, her eyes narrowing even further.

Graham shifted, for the sendoff she was giving was perfectly clear. He wasn't accustomed to such a thing. Chaperones always liked dukes. There was hardly a better thing for their charges to land.

But Lady Opal looked heated and Adelaide looked slightly sick as she stared at him, her gaze telling him without words that if he left it would make it easier on her.

So he bowed again. "Well, I should be off and leave you two to your walk. I hope I shall have the pleasure of your company again, ladies."

"Goodbye, Gr—Your Grace," Adelaide said softly. Her aunt merely sniffed and Graham remounted and urged his horse onward down the path. But he couldn't help a quick glance back toward Adelaide.

Nor could he ignore the fact that during the moments he'd

stood with her, he hadn't once thought of Lydia. And he wasn't thinking of her now as he carried on, wondering at Lady Opal's coldness and at the pleasure he took in spending even just a moment with her charge.

"What is your trouble today?"

Graham stared at the note written in Ewan's even handwriting and tried to collect himself before he looked up into his friend's face. They were sitting in Graham's office together and he knew he wasn't good company. His mind was too…wild. He couldn't seem to rein it in from wandering to thoughts of soft skin, blonde hair, and a night that was unlike anything he'd ever encountered in his nearly three decades on this earth.

That was one trouble. The other was more complicated. Because he also couldn't stop thinking of another woman, this one with a sharp wit and unexpected insight. One who could and *did* easily set him down like he wasn't a duke. Like he was just a man. And he liked it.

It had been two days since he'd seen either of them, but they both dominated his thoughts. His dreams. Sometimes they even merged together in a most troubling and erotic fashion.

He met Ewan's eyes and saw nothing but calm and gentle and trustworthy friendship in them. He'd always been able to talk to him, even sometimes more than James and Simon. And it wasn't just because his muteness kept him from interrupting. It was that Ewan truly listened. *Heard.*

"Do I have a trouble?" he asked. Ewan didn't write anything but screwed up his face in an exasperated expression that said everything. Graham laughed despite himself and said, "Well, I *might* have a problem, I suppose."

Ewan wrote, *"Which is?"*

"I-I…" He hesitated, for the moment he said the next words out loud, he was going to have to face them. Really face them.

"I want two women."

Ewan's eyes bugged and he opened and shut his mouth a few times before he slowly took his pad back and wrote, "Well, I suppose I should be happy you want to get back into the world. Though you certainly don't waste time. I guess you and Roseford could talk about that."

Graham stiffened. "No, I don't mean two women the way Roseford likes to have two women. Anyway, I thought Roseford was more interested in sharing a woman with a friend. His friend, not hers. Either way, that isn't what I'm talking about."

Ewan shrugged, and it was the indication that Graham should continue.

"I mean, I'm attracted to two *different* women." Now the words were out and he recognized how true they were.

Ewan scribbled, "I assume one is the actress?"

"Yes," Graham said, running a hand through his hair. "Lydia Ford. Was I so obvious?"

Ewan nodded and Graham laughed again.

"Yes, I suppose I was that first night you and Tyndale took me to the theatre. But it's gone beyond a mere distant attraction. I went to her again two nights ago." He shook his head. "And I...I couldn't resist her anymore. We...well, we did what you would expect we'd do."

He could have given more details, but he chose not to. Ewan wasn't the type to want to know about the women his friends bedded. Even if he were, Graham felt reluctant to share this time. What had happened with Lydia was powerful, special. If he talked about it to a friend, it felt like cheapening the night.

Cheapening her.

"She has secrets," he said instead. "I feel them. And I know that she's also doing something that isn't exactly safe, so I feel this desire to protect her."

Ewan's expression softened and he nodded as he wrote, *"You would, though."*

Graham flinched. Only a handful of his friends knew the truth of his past. James, Simon...Ewan. And Kit, who had once kept Graham from actually murdering his own father. But every time he was reminded that someone had a glimpse into his true soul, it made him uncomfortable.

Ewan seemed to sense his reluctance to continue that line of discussion and scribbled, *"Who is the other woman who has your attention?"*

He sighed. "It's, er, Lady Adelaide. She's the daughter of the late Earl of Longford. Emma's good friend."

Ewan just stared at him, making no move to write anything at all. Graham shifted as the silence stretched out. Then Ewan very slowly and deliberately wrote, *"The wallflower.* You *want a wallflower?"*

Graham ground his teeth. "First, you should talk, duke who never goes to a damned party. If there was ever a male wallflower, it's *you.*"

Ewan glared at him, but waved him to continue.

"And the fact is, she is more than just that silly label." He got up and paced away from Ewan. "She's intelligent and direct. To a fault with both. She wears her hair too tight and I'm not even sure she needs those spectacles that block her eyes so you're not really certain what's going on in her mind."

Talking about her made him picture her and his gut tightened as he continued, "She's a wonderful dancer though she never does it, which makes her too like me. She's frustrating beyond measure because sometimes I feel she is willfully misunderstanding me. She's not my type, you're right about that. She's not my type, though to be honest, I really don't know what my 'type' is anymore. Regardless of all that I…*like* her. And if I'm honest with myself, I want her."

He sank back into his chair and let the full effect of that statement hit him. He'd spent a powerful night making love to Lydia, and yet less than forty-eight hours later he could admit that he wanted Adelaide, as well.

He liked both of them. He desired both of them. And that was highly uncomfortable. After all, he had been suffering the past few months because of a betrayal of loyalty. But where was the loyalty in these complicated feelings that now brewed inside of him?

"That is a pickle," Ewan wrote, summarizing Graham's issue in one rather dismissive line.

Graham nearly threw the notepad back at him. "So helpful, Donburrow, really. That clears it up, I'll just go about my business."

Ewan was laughing now, a rare act that shook his body even if it was noiseless and brightened his usually somber face. *"I'm sorry,"* he wrote, his handwriting shaky from his humor. *"What do you wish me to say?"*

"Tell me what to do?" Graham said with a shake of his head. "You're so much bloody smarter than the rest of us put together, you must have a thought."

Ewan's expression changed, just a flash of emotion before he smoothed it away. He was still a moment, then he wrote, "Connection isn't the place where I'm particularly clever, but it seems to me that you are missing pieces in your relationship with each of these women. With Lydia, you don't know her secrets. Her true personality or life. And with Adelaide she keeps you at a distance physically. Like the glasses you say she wears that she doesn't need. A barrier, yes? A line she won't let you cross?"

"You really *are* the smartest of us," Graham muttered. "Yes, I think that's it. There is a boundary between each of us. Are you suggesting that I cross those boundaries with each woman?"

Ewan nodded.

"And what happens if I still want both of them?" he asked as he tried to picture kissing Adelaide the same way he kissed Lydia. Finding he could do it quite easily and hating himself for it.

Ewan shrugged. "Then come back and we'll talk about it some more."

Graham bent his head. He'd spent his life, at least his life up until the past few months, always being certain of what he did. Now he wasn't certain of anything.

And he wasn't sure if that was freeing or horrifying. He would likely have to decide before he approached either woman again.

CHAPTER TEN

Adelaide stepped from the stage and handed off the prop sword that had been her character's demise to Toby. He took it with a brief smile and said, "You've flowers that came during the show again. That duke does seem to like you."

Adelaide returned his smile, but her stomach dropped with the mention of Graham. He might very well have sent her flowers. She would not have put it past him. But he'd made no effort to speak to her in nearly a week, not as Lydia nor as Adelaide. She'd looked for him at each of her performances and she'd sought him out in various ballrooms since, but he was not to be found.

And she had a horrible sense of loss at that thought. One that made her frown draw down as she entered her dressing room and shut the door behind her. Her head ached, her makeup made her skin feel stretched and she just wanted to go home to her bed.

The offending flowers were sitting on her table waiting for her. Hot house roses, thick with scent and bright with happy color. They almost mocked her as she stared at them with their note that simply read *To Lydia, From G.*

She glanced in the mirror as she sank into the seat to remove her makeup. She looked as drawn as she felt, and she hesitated as she stared at herself.

"You were meaningless," she murmured to herself. "No matter what name you went by. You were *meaningless* and he is finished with you, despite how many bouquets he sends."

She let out a sigh and briefly covered her eyes with her fingers. When she gathered herself and lowered them, she gasped. In the reflection she saw Sir Archibald standing behind her. Somehow he had slipped into her room without making a sound, and now he had shut himself in.

She jumped up and faced him. The man was round and red and had a cruel bent to his expression. And he was obsessed with the theatre. Well, perhaps not the theatre itself. She doubted he could tell Shakespeare from a supper menu, but he was obsessed with actresses. How many of her friends had told teary-eyed tales of his groping hands and hard, unyielding mouth?

Currently he was obsessed with Melinda, Adelaide's understudy, as had been proven by Melinda's hiding from his grasping hands and mouth days ago. But his desire for the other woman didn't stop Sir Archibald from looking *her* up and down with leering eyes.

"Lydia," he drawled. "I was searching for Matilda, but you look lovely."

"Melinda," Adelaide corrected softly, thinking of her friend's terror as she cowered in the dressing room just a week before. She was glad Sir Archibald hadn't found Melinda first.

"Same difference," he said with an ugly sneer. "You're all the same to me."

"She isn't here," Adelaide said. "And I'm surprised to find *you* here. I thought you had been asked not to come back during or after performances anymore."

Toby had been the one to do that. And how he had managed to do it civilly when he'd been so enraged at Sir Archibald's treatment of Melinda was beyond her.

"That pup doesn't run me, Lydia," Sir Archibald said, taking a step toward her. "I know the man who owns this theatre, you know. I'll have that manager on the street in a heartbeat if I see fit."

Adelaide swallowed hard. Men like Sir Archibald could threaten those with so much to lose. She was different, of course.

She had a life to go back to that had nothing to do with performing. Such as it was.

"You are not welcome here by *any* of us," she said, forcing her tone to be hard and firm even when she felt as terrified as a deer being run down by a wolf. "And I would think that the theatre would be more interested in the money it brings in with actresses like me than with one nasty man's opinion."

Sir Archibald's face hardened in an instant. "You whore, don't you act for a second like you're more important than I am."

He swung on her, the back of his hand cracking across her cheek and staggering her back against the chair she had vacated upon his intrusion. She was made so off balance by the attack that she had no recourse when Sir Archibald threw himself up against her and backed her against the table.

Her mind began to spin as she shoved against him, clawing his fat belly and kicking at him as his thick fingers clenched her dress. She heard the fabric beginning to rend as he dropped his mouth to hers and slobbered a disgusting kiss against her tightly pressed lips.

"No!" she cried out, but her voice was muffled as he continued to cover her mouth with his own. "No!" she repeated.

But he was an immoveable object, nearly twice her weight, and she recognized in that horrible moment that it was very likely he would do whatever he wanted, however he wanted, long before anyone would come to her aid.

Graham came up the long hallway toward Lydia's dressing room with a spring in his step. He couldn't wait to see her, even if his thoughts about her were still tangled. He'd stayed away for days, trying to see if his attraction to either woman would fade if he avoided them a while.

It had not. So he'd chosen to come here first, to see Lydia and try to connect with her in some way that was deeper than the physical. Try to see into her secrets.

As he neared her door, he heard a soft sound from behind it. A muffled cry of pain, and he caught his breath before he barged forward and crashed through into the dressing room.

What he saw there froze his blood. Sir Archibald, a man who was far too well-known to him, loomed over Lydia, wiping his mouth over her as she struggled to keep him at bay. The shoulder of her gown was torn and the fabric gaped forward as the brute cupped one breast and squeezed.

A red veil of rage settled over Graham's vision. Unstoppable, uncontrollable and driven by more than a mere desire to help Lydia, Graham careened forward and caught Sir Archibald by the lapels to fling him off of Lydia. His mind went blank of reason. Replaced by thoughts of another woman being hurt, another set of angry hands, another life he tried desperately to forget as often as possible.

He rained down fists on Sir Archibald's fat face, crushing him over and over without speaking, without hesitating, without thinking. He only wanted to destroy.

"Graham!" He heard Lydia's voice behind him, loud and filled with pleading. He ignored it.

"Graham!" she said again, but this time it was Adelaide's voice that spoke to him.

He felt her hands close around his arm and pull with all her weight. The touch cleared his mind and his vision, and he stopped, fist cocked back and looked down at Sir Archibald.

The man was covered in blood and his nose was broken. Perhaps his jaw too, given how swollen his cheek was. He sputtered, his hands lifted to protect himself, his eyes wide with fear even though they were starting to swell shut.

"Graham."

He turned and it was Lydia who held him. Not Adelaide. He'd just been confused. She stared at him in horror and empathy, but didn't release his arm.

"Stop," she said softly. "Stop now."

He became aware of other things in the room now. A

gathering of people was at the door, staring at him like he was a monster. He looked down at himself. His jacket had blood on it, his waistcoat, even his cravat. And his hand hurt. His knuckles had split open sometime during the relentless assault, and they bled just like Sir Archibald's face bled.

"Lydia," he whispered. His ears began to ring as he looked at her horrified expression to his knuckles to Sir Archibald's swelling face. And a wave of horror overcame him.

He was out of control. He was violent. He was everything he'd always fought not to be.

In that horrible moment, he was his father.

Adelaide all but pushed Graham into her little carriage, and he didn't resist. She had never seen anyone like he was in that moment, blank, numb, mechanical. He staggered against the carriage seat and leaned there, staring straight ahead as she gave a quick direction to her driver, climbed in across from him and the vehicle began to move.

She looked at her seat beside her and flinched. Her Adelaide gown was sitting there, waiting for her. She always changed in her carriage on the way home. It was a thirty-minute drive, long enough to transform herself back into Adelaide from Lydia.

If Graham recognized the gown…

But he continued to stare at nothing, his silence and the pain on his handsome face keeping her from worrying about anything but him. She drew a deep breath and gently moved to the opposite side of the vehicle beside him.

"Graham," she said softly.

He jolted a little, like he'd forgotten she was there. He turned his gaze down toward her and his vision cleared slightly.

"Lydia," he whispered, and his voice was like nothing she'd ever heard before. "I'm sorry."

Tears flooded her eyes as she stared at him. This man was

broken. Not broken like everyone thought he'd been after the betrayal of the Duke of Crestwood. This was something different. Something deeper. This was something she doubted he had ever allowed any other person to see, even those friends who he loved so deeply.

This was a glimpse into the soft underbelly of a man who was nothing but muscle and bone and sinew. *This* was what he fought to hide.

She saw it all. And she knew it was a gift. Not one he meant to give, perhaps, but a gift nonetheless. That it was given to Lydia, someone who wasn't real…that was something to be faced another day.

"You have nothing to be sorry about," she soothed him. "You came to my aid. You saved me."

He shook his head slowly. "I saw him hurting you and I went…blank. I went back in time." His voice broke and he turned away from her to stare back out the window. She didn't push. Not yet. She just reached across and took his hand, resting it in her lap as she smoothed her fingertips across his damaged knuckles.

The rest of the ride was silent. She wanted so much to talk to him, to press him, but she didn't. Not in her carriage. It didn't feel safe to do it here. She waited until they stopped in front of Graham's big townhouse. The same place where he'd made love to her so sweetly.

Now she stepped out of the carriage and turned back, holding out her hand to him as she ignored the servants who came rushing to help. He took her hand, staring down at her with an intensity that was sudden and powerful. She forced herself to hold that stare, praying he would see her support, her trustworthiness.

Praying he wouldn't see a fact that had become very clear to her the moment he rushed into the room to save her. She was beginning to care for this man. Deeply. Powerfully. She feared how strong those feelings were, especially considering the dangerous line she was treading between reality and fiction.

One Graham didn't even know existed.

"Come," she said as they moved toward the house together.

His butler hurried down the steps as they moved toward the front door, and she could see from the look of surprise and concern on the stern man's face that he was as stricken by the expression of his master as she was. "Your Grace?"

Graham lifted his gaze slightly. "It's fine, Rogers. I'm...I'm fine. Mrs. Ford will assist me."

The butler's gaze came to her and she met his eyes. It was almost impossible to do so, knowing what he would see. Knowing what he'd judge her as. But he merely nodded. "May I...may I do anything, Mrs. Ford?"

She smiled at his kindness and his loyalty to Graham. "I'll need some towels," she said softly. "Perhaps a bit of whiskey."

"Yes, miss," he said with another quick nod before he stepped off to arrange everything.

"I don't want whiskey," Graham said as they started up the stairs together toward his room. She recalled every step toward it from the last time they'd been there. What a very different walk that had been, with charged excitement in the air around them.

"It isn't to drink," she said softly as she opened his chamber door and led him in. "Your knuckles are injured. I'll clean the wounds with some whiskey."

He staggered toward the fire, shrugging out of his jacket as he did so. He dropped it behind him without looking and then went to work on his waistcoat. She heard him suck in breath through his teeth, and she moved toward him.

"Let me," she whispered. "Your hands are bruised."

She reached him in a few steps and touched his bicep to turn him. She felt the muscle tighten beneath her fingers and he stared down at her, expression unreadable as she lifted her hands to unfasten his buttons. He caught her fingers before she could.

"I'm bloody," he ground out. "I don't want to...to sully you with what I did tonight."

She shook her head. "There is no sullying, Graham." She

92

shook his grip off and unfastened his waistcoat. He was right, there was blood on the fabric and the buttons. She winced as it slid across her skin, proof of the violence that had brought this man to his knees in a way she'd never expected.

Men fought all the time, didn't they? But Graham had lost control. This was the consequence. She didn't understand it. But she was terrified of it.

When the buttons were parted, he pulled the vest away. She would have gone to work on his cravat and his shirt, but there was a light knock at the door. She turned away from him and moved to answer, finding Rogers there with a tray containing a pitcher of water, a bottle of whiskey and a pile of small towels.

"Will there be anything else?" he asked.

She shook her head. "No. Thank you."

He glanced past her into the room, his face drawn with concern, but then he nodded and she closed the door. She moved to the table beside Graham's window and set the items there, then filled the small basin on another table with the clean water. She took a towel and dipped it into the water. As she turned toward him, she found he had already managed out of his bloody shirt on his own and had dropped it with the rest.

She caught her breath, taken in by how beautiful he was, just as she had been the last time she'd been here with him. Tonight, though, his expression was far different. Gone was the predatory, confident, sensual man who would seduce her.

And what was left was something painful, someone she very much wanted to console and protect and heal.

"Come here," she said, motioning to the chair beside the table.

He did as she asked, sinking into the chair and watching as she lifted one hand and began to gently wash the combination of his blood and Sir Archibald's away. He winced as she did so, but didn't try to pull away or stop him.

"I hit Simon," he said softly after a silence that had seemed to stretch out forever.

She lifted her gaze to him, searching his face with renewed

concern. "No, darling. Not Simon. You hit Sir Archibald, it wasn't your friend."

Graham shook his head slowly. "Not tonight. I-I hit Simon when I found him with Meg. I broke his nose. Like Archibald's. I looked down tonight and I saw Simon's face for a moment and I thought—"

He cut himself off and jerked his hand from her grip before he got up and paced away from her. The muscles in his shoulders rippled as he dragged a hand through his hair, freeing it from the queue so it fell around his handsome face.

She clenched her hands in her lap, willing herself not to get up, not to go to him. To just let him speak. She could feel the dam of whatever he held inside straining. It was bound to break. At least with her...with Lydia...he would be safe.

She would make certain of it.

"I think you could be forgiven for punching Simon after how he betrayed you," she said softly.

"You don't understand," he whispered. "It wasn't that I hit him. It was that this...thing rose up in me. This...*thing*. This angry, cruel, out of control thing. I reined it in that day, but tonight I couldn't. Tonight it broke free. If you hadn't caught my arm, Lydia, I would have killed that man. I wouldn't have stopped until he was dead."

She rose at last, setting the bloody cloth back into the basin before she took a tentative step toward him. He flinched even at that barest movement so she stilled immediately. She drew in a few breaths, fighting for calm because she knew he needed it.

"Graham, you stopped him from attacking me," she said.

"I could have thrown him off of you and stopped him," Graham said. "I may have grabbed him for the good and honorable reason of staying his attack, but I pummeled him because I wanted to. Because I felt good while I was doing it. Because I'm *him*."

Her brow wrinkled, for she was truly confused. "Him who?" she asked slowly. "Him, Sir Archibald? Him, Simon?"

All the air left Graham's lungs and he was perfectly still for a moment. Then he lifted blue eyes so clear and perfect that her chest hurt when she looked into them. He held her gaze, unblinking, unwavering, and said, "I'm my father."

She saw it all so plainly then. Saw a glimpse, brief but bared, of a little boy with blond hair and blue eyes, one that had seen a monster, a real monster, and now the man before her feared that the monster had returned. She saw what no one in Society knew or had ever whispered about.

She saw the truth of Graham Everly, Duke of Northfield, and she choked on her grief for him. For whatever he had seen and gone through.

"Tell me about him," she said, moving a step closer. He didn't back away this time, and she was grateful for that. She didn't touch him yet, though, and he seemed equally grateful.

She watched his throat work, she watched the pain on every line of his face. Then he choked out, "No one knows the truth."

She nodded. "I imagined as much."

When she said nothing more, he jerked his gaze to her. "There were a few who knew that he beat me," he said. "James, Kit, Ewan...*Simon*. That was why I've always been so protective, like tonight."

She smiled softly. "Protective is not a bad trait in a man with so much power, you know. It is far better than the alternative."

"Perhaps," he conceded slowly. "But protective didn't save me when I was eight and he broke my arm. Protective didn't save me when he scarred my shoulder with a cigar when I was eleven."

She winced. She'd seen those little scars on his skin and written them off as the typical bumps and knocks an active man would find for himself. Now they took on a sinister edge, marks that indicated the strength of him in character, not just in body. He had endured.

And Adelaide understood a bit of that, herself.

"Protective didn't keep him from—" He broke off and bent his head, his shoulders slumping slightly. They began to shake.

"What did he do?" she asked.

He lifted his gaze once more, but he was looking past her now. Through her. Into a time and place she couldn't see. Something she wasn't sure she *wanted* to see. But she pushed anyway, because this was no longer about what she needed. It was about the man across from her.

"He...he murdered my mother."

CHAPTER ELEVEN

Graham watched as horror and heartbreak played across Lydia's delicate features. And there was empathy, too, a tiny understanding that he wasn't certain most in his life would feel. This woman had endured something. *That* was what he was supposed to find out about tonight.

Instead he stood before her, stripped half naked in body and fully naked in soul. And yet saying that horrible thing out loud somehow felt…better.

"Graham," she whispered at last. He could see how much she wanted to rush to him. To touch him, to hold him. But she didn't. For his sake. To allow him this moment without trying to crowd it out of him, and he appreciated that, too.

"She was lovely," he said. "Quiet and kind, gentle to all around her. She used to tousle my hair when she didn't think *he* was looking. She called me Gig—I guess that's what I used to call myself when I was learning to talk. My father hated that. He said she was making me soft and weak. He had to make me strong. He had a very specific way of doing that."

Lydia swallowed hard. "With his fists."

He nodded once, pain flooding every part of him. He could stop now. He could see that if he did she wouldn't push him. She would let him back away from the past he never spoke of to anyone. And yet he couldn't. Now that the ball had begun to roll down this long and dangerous hill, he couldn't call it back. He had to let it crash as it would, at the bottom.

Perhaps it was better that way.

"I always knew he hit her. We were a pair, the two of us. She'd throw herself in front of me and eventually I started throwing myself in front of her. Protecting each other. Only there was no protection from that...*monster* who paraded around like he was a godly man. A good man. A decent man who was liked by those who thought they knew him."

He shook his head and caught a glimpse of his bruised knuckles. Evidence that perhaps he was no better than that wolf who'd masqueraded as a sheep. He'd lost control, like he'd seen his father do so many times.

"What happened?" she pressed, drawing him back out of his musings. But to no better place.

His breathing rasped in the quiet around them. His battered hands shook. "I was seven years old. I'd broken something—a dish, perhaps. An accident. And he lost all control and reason. He came at me across a room like a bull in a paddock and I froze, utterly terrified. He was so fucking big, Lydia. He felt like he was ten feet tall, with a fist the size of a ham. He was screaming, almost incoherent with rage. And she stepped between us, trying to stop him, to calm him."

He stopped because the room around him was fading, replaced by images of another room, another night. Replaced by the sounds of his mother screaming as his father's fists rained down on her slight body. Of the screams stopping suddenly and heartbreakingly. Of his father turning on him, his hands bloody just like Graham's had been earlier in the night.

He could still remember what he'd said next, "You will come to heel, boy. Or you'll end up buried next to her."

Lydia gasped and Graham blinked, back in this room. He realized he'd been speaking out loud, reciting what he saw in that state. Lydia's hand was pressed so hard into her mouth that her knuckles were white, her eyes were wide as saucers. Tears streamed down over her cheeks and her fingers as she stared at him in voiceless and helpless pain.

"She died two days later. He told everyone that it was a

sudden illness. And he sent me away to school soon after. Eventually I met Simon and James and the rest, and I hid with them as much as I could. One day I just got too big to push."

She moved toward him now, her hand outstretched. How he wanted to let her touch him, to let her comfort him as he could see she would. To let her fold herself around him and fill the gaping emptiness that he had carried forever.

Only he knew there was some part of him that couldn't be filled. And he backed away.

"Don't," he said softly. "Not after tonight."

"And what does tonight have to do with your mother's death at the hands of a monster? Or what he did to you in the years before and after?" she said, her voice tight.

He shook his head as he looked at her. "You know what, Lydia. You saw me. You stopped me. You *know* what I was doing."

"Defending me!" she snapped, but there was something in her tone that told him she knew the truth.

He barked out an ugly sound. "No, Lydia. I was the monster tonight. I was my father."

She sucked in her breath between her teeth and now she charged forward again, beautiful and light and completely unafraid despite what she'd heard and seen. He found himself leaning toward her, incapable of drawing back one more time.

She caught his arm, holding tight as she stared up into his face. "You were *nothing* like your father. Not tonight, not ever," she insisted.

"You who have known me, what, a fortnight?" he said, but he still didn't pull away from the comfort Lydia offered. Now that he'd spilled all he was to her, he had no strength to fight anymore.

He would be selfish, because that was what his father had put in his blood.

Her face twisted at his question, and for a moment he saw something in her gaze. Something…guilty. But then it was gone.

"Perhaps I haven't known you, *truly* known you, for very

long," she said softly. "But I *do* know you, Graham. What you did tonight, what you did when you struck Simon, those things don't make you your father."

She moved even closer, brushing his hair back from his face. The air began to leave the room as she locked eyes with him. And his need to have her close began to transform into something with more purpose and heat.

"Ewan said I needed your secrets," he confessed as she brushed her thumb over his lower lip. "And here I gave you mine, didn't I?"

Adelaide froze, her finger still heavy on his full lips as she stared up into his eyes. Secrets. He'd been on a mission to find her secrets when his own painful past had fallen from those same lips she touched now.

And her own secrets felt so damned heavy right now. So painful.

She stepped back a little. "You—you spoke to a friend about me?" she asked, pretending that she didn't know that Ewan was Ewan Hoffstead, the infamous Silent Duke of Donburrow.

Graham nodded slowly. "I did. And—"

He cut himself off, and she fought the urge to groan out her frustration. That he would speak to a friend about Lydia Ford was meaningful. He wanted to be closer to this character she had created.

She was thrilled and horrified by that fact in equal measure.

"And?" she pushed, needing to know what he would say next.

He caught her wrist and smoothed a thumb across the delicate bones there. "I did, that's all," he said.

Her heart had begun to throb already, but as he drew her a little closer it pounded like a wild stallion set free. She was in dangerous waters beyond her wildest imaginings now. The wrong move and she might very well drown.

A fate that didn't seem all so terrible when he lowered his lips to hers and she tasted the sweetness of his kiss and the pulsing heat of his desire behind it. But there was something more there tonight. He needed her. Not just physically, as had existed between them in the past.

He needed her comfort. Her presence. Her touch. Only he needed all that in the guise of Lydia Ford. She pushed aside the pain of that fact once more and sank into his kiss, winding her arms around his neck and gently stroking her tongue into his mouth.

He sighed, the sound shuddering from his lips as his arms came around her waist and he held there, almost sagging from what she knew was emotional exhaustion. She knew it all too well.

Gently, she guided him backward, toward his bed. When they reached it, she broke the kiss and looked up at him. "Will you let me take care of you tonight?" she whispered.

Emotion flashed over his face once more, and he said, "Do I deserve such pleasure?"

She nodded. "In my mind you do. And mine is the only opinion that matters, isn't it?"

A tiny smile tilted his lips. A shadow of his normal knowing, wicked grin, which he only seemed to gift Lydia. But the fact that there was any pleasure to be had for him buoyed her determination to offer him this comfort.

"Who am I to argue with a lady?" he asked.

She stiffened slightly. A lady? Oh, he didn't know the half of it. She stepped back. "Remove the rest then and up onto the pillows you go."

He stared at her. "And what will you do, Lydia?"

She put her back to him and drew a deep breath before she began to unfasten her torn costume. She was pleased to be in it at present, for it was easy to remove on her own, designed so she could quickly alter her look in the wings of the stage between acts or scenes.

"You worry about yourself, Your Grace. I'll worry about me," she tossed over her shoulder.

She faced him as she unbuttoned the last button and smiled. For all his arguing, he had removed his clothing as she'd asked and now lay across his bed in all his naked glory. Oh, and there was glory to it. He truly was magnificent, a beautiful specimen of the best a man could be. Muscled and toned and hard and hers.

She shimmied the dress away slowly and stood before him, as naked as he was. He caught his breath, a loud inhalation in the quiet room, but he made no move to touch her or control what was happening. Perhaps he was too exhausted by what he'd shared. Or perhaps he just wanted to surrender to her tonight.

Either way she felt a swell of power that this man who could control any situation or person within his reach would concede any quarter to her. That took trust. A trust she most certainly hadn't earned considering all the ways she was lying to him.

He sat up on his elbows and tilted his head. "You're thinking, Lydia."

She smiled slightly at his easy read of her turbulent mind. "Am I? And what's wrong with that?"

"Nothing except I want you to be busy touching me, not analyzing everything that is happening." Now he did reach out a hand, but his blue eyes didn't leave her face. "Please."

The *please* was said so softly and with so much need that she couldn't resist it. Slowly she climbed onto the bed and crawled toward him. She ignored his outstretched hand as she caged him in with an arm on either side of his head. Her hair fell down around them in a curtain and her body brushed his as she lowered her lips and kissed him once more.

He opened to her with a soft sigh, and she took and took and took, drinking deeply of this man who so enthralled and captivated and frustrated and terrified her. This man who she had tried to avoid for most of her life and now she couldn't get enough of.

This man she wanted beyond reason, even though she

couldn't truly have him, not in either life she had created for herself, as Lydia or as Adelaide. He was out of reach, stolen from time.

And in that moment she didn't give a damn. She gently straddled him as she continued to kiss him, feeling the hard thrust of his erection pressed between her legs. But she didn't take him, even though she was slick and ready and aching for him. No, tonight was about comfort. She hadn't even begun to offer that yet.

She dragged her mouth away from his, sliding down his body. She'd had experience before, of course. She hadn't been a virgin the first night Graham touched her. But what she'd done back then was nothing like what she shared with him. She was driven to touch him, to hold him, to taste him, to take him into her body. Her needs controlled her as she kissed along his shoulders, his collarbone, and finally dragged her tongue across his nipple just like he had done to her so many times.

He arched slightly under her ministrations, his muscles rippling beneath her touch as his eyes came shut and he groaned her name under his breath. Only it *wasn't* her name, and Adelaide flinched at the evidence of the falsehood she had so carefully crafted.

Then she forced those thoughts away and surrendered herself to Lydia. She dragged her fingers down his stomach, tracing a pattern with her nails across his skin before she gently cupped his cock and stroked it once, twice. He lifted his hips into her with a garbled curse, and she smiled against his skin.

Pleasuring this man was the gift of a lifetime. Not for him, for herself. She would surely remember every single one of these moments long after this thing between them was over. But she refused to think of the end. She focused on this moment.

And dragged her lips even lower. His skin tasted like man and heat and Graham. She memorized every flavor as she licked his hip and then found herself face to face with his cock.

She looked up at him and found him staring down, his eyes wide and filled with breathless anticipation.

"You don't have to," he grunted.

She smiled at him. "I don't have to do anything, Your Grace."

Then she lowered her mouth over him and took him inside. She'd heard her friends at the theatre talk about this act. She'd even walked in on a lightskirt performing it on another actor once, so she wasn't entirely uninformed. But seeing and hearing were very different from doing. She wasn't fully ready for the hard and soft of Graham against her tongue, filling her mouth as far as she could take him.

She also wasn't prepared for the pulse of hot and heavy need that cascaded through her, setting her on fire as she began to take him. His hands fisted against the coverlet and his neck dipped back, revealing the veins and tendons there. She watched him as she took him with her mouth, slowing her strokes when he moaned, adding her tongue when he seemed to like it, gently fisting the length she couldn't manage to take into her throat.

She could feel him easing toward the brink. She wanted to push him over, to give this man pleasure without asking for anything in return. But he was Graham. Of course he wouldn't allow for that.

He sat up and caught her arms, pulling her mouth away as he dragged her up his body and smashed his lips to hers. She slid over him, straddling him once more, and cried out with pleasure as he speared into her body with one long thrust.

His kisses were desperate and needy, but so were hers. She began to grind over him, her body clawing for pleasure, milking him for his as his fingers dug into her bare hips and moved her harder and faster over him. She threw her head back as the orgasm flamed through her, jolted her hips without control.

He pushed hard up into her, and then he cried out and she felt his seed spill into her body before he flopped back against the pillows, dragging her still twitching body over his where he held her like he would never let her go.

Adelaide lay on her side facing Graham. He was sprawled on his stomach, his face turned toward her, gentle in sleep. She was doing a math problem in her head. A calculation of how deep a mistake she had made tonight. Graham had spent inside of her. Not a problem, perhaps, for a woman like Lydia Ford. A woman like that could leverage a child into a windfall from a man like this. He'd pay to protect her child. She would go on as before.

No one would be hurt.

Only Lydia Ford didn't exist. Lady Adelaide did. And if her math problem wasn't correct, she would end up swollen with a child, ruined forever, perhaps out on the street if her aunt reacted as poorly as she had the last time Adelaide had fallen. And that time it had been private. Easy to hide.

Only the math in her head told her that a child was not very likely. So perhaps there was nothing to fear.

Except that she had gone too far with Graham tonight. Not because of making love. Because he had given her so much of his soul. *Lydia.* He'd given Lydia his soul.

Adelaide reached out and traced a small, pale scar on Graham's ribcage near his back. He stirred slightly but didn't wake as she stared at the mark that proved the pain he had confessed to her hours before.

She rose and quietly dressed herself as she continued to stare at the remarkable, wonderful man on the bed. The one she was lying to. She had to tell him the truth. That was clear.

Only she didn't know how. He would be devastated when he realized the wallflower he thought nothing of was the one who had seduced his secrets from him. And what of the nights they'd spent together? He was a decent man, an honorable man. If he thought there was a chance she could be breeding, he might even force a marriage.

Her heart thrilled at that briefly, but she shoved it aside. She would never force him to marry her. So perhaps she could wait. Wait until after her courses came. Then she could tell him without hesitation there was no child.

And whatever consequences that came after, she would bear. He would hate her and she'd take that. She'd earned it, after all. And she'd still know that she'd had him, if only briefly.

If only because of a lie.

CHAPTER TWELVE

Graham paced his bedroom, glancing occasionally at the rumpled bed where he'd awoken alone an hour ago. In his hand, he gripped a note from Lydia, left for him to find that morning. A simple line that said she wanted him to rest, that she would see him again soon.

Part of him was thrilled that she wasn't just walking away after hearing the truth of him. But there was another part that felt...uneasy. Uneasy because thoughts of Adelaide continued to crowd his mind. How would she react if she knew he had given so much of himself, body and soul, to another woman?

He'd been faithful to Meg, who he hadn't cared for beyond friendship. He wasn't involved with Adelaide in any official capacity. He hadn't even kissed her. And yet he felt he'd betrayed her with Lydia.

His mind spun. And he needed a friend. Tyndale had been called out of town. Ewan was packing up for his country estate— he meant to spend Christmas there, so he was going weeks and weeks early to prepare everything. An excuse, Graham knew, to escape the city he hated.

Still neither of them was available for him at present. And so that left James.

James had always been one of Graham's closest friends. He and Simon had started out together, before the others. Before the club. Before their titles and their responsibilities. Their friendship had been damaged by everything that had happened in the summer, but he still wanted James's opinion. His help.

Actually, it *wasn't* James he wished to speak to. It was Simon. Simon, who could see into the heart of an issue and speak plainly without being cruel.

Only Simon was...well, Graham still wasn't ready to face him yet. So James it would be.

He'd have to tread carefully. James knew some of the abuse he'd suffered at the hands of his father, as had some of the others. But Graham had never told anyone the secret about his mother's death.

Until Lydia.

He winced as he relived the previous night once more. Then he pushed the thoughts from his mind and moved to his door. He rang the bell there and waited less than patiently for the footman who answered the call.

"Your Grace?" the young man said between out of breath gasps from jogging to respond.

"Tell Walters to be ready, as I'm penning a missive to the Duke of Abernathe that I'll need to be delivered as soon as possible," he said. "And let Rogers know I likely will be dining with Abernathe and the duchess tonight, so there should be no special preparations made for supper."

"Yes, sir," the servant said. "I'll return shortly to retrieve your message."

Graham acknowledged his words with a nod and then closed the door. It was rude to invite oneself to supper, even to a friend's. But he needed to see James. And after they ate, he intended to explain everything going on in his life.

Maybe he could sort it out for himself even as he tried to explain it.

Adelaide paced the parlor, waiting for her aunt to join her

for their usual afternoon tea. Normally she would run lines while she waited, but her mind was not on that. No, she couldn't stop thinking about Graham. What they'd shared, what he'd told her, what she, herself was withholding from him.

She felt horrible. But she couldn't veer from her course. She would wait another week, wait until her courses came, then she would reveal herself and let the consequences come.

"Oh God, I hope I can do it," she whispered as she stopped to stare out the window to the street below. A goodly part of her wanted to jump out and just run.

But that wasn't possible. Not for a woman like her. To do that would be to give up Adelaide forever. And there was more Adelaide in her than Lydia. She wasn't brave enough to surrender to the character she'd created in an act of desperation.

She heard the door behind her shut and turned. Her aunt was standing at the barrier now, arms folded and her thin, wrinkled face lined with…anger.

Adelaide shoved the rest of her thoughts of Graham aside and readied herself for the worst. After all, she knew that look so very well.

"Aunt Opal," she said, forcing her tone to be light as she carefully edged toward the sideboard where the tea was ready. "Right on time, as always. May I pour you some tea? And Mrs. Bligh has prepared your very favorite cakes, I see. I know you'll want one of those."

"I know you're lying to me," Opal said, ignoring the questions.

Adelaide had been reaching for the teapot and her hands froze midway. She swallowed hard, past her fear and slowly turned to her aunt.

"About the cakes?" she said, as breezy as Lydia delivering a line. "I assure you, I'm not. Come see for yourself."

Her aunt slammed her hand back against the door. "Not about the cakes, you stupid girl. I know you're lying to me. I recognize the signs from *last time*."

She hissed out the last two words, and Adelaide flinched at

the wretched sound. At the memories her words evoked.

"You're imagining things," she whispered.

Both her aunt's eyebrows lifted at once and she moved toward Adelaide like a snake, coiled and ready to strike with poison dripping from its fangs.

Only Opal's poison would be with her words, her cruelty.

Adelaide briefly wished it would be real venom rather than the kind that scarred the soul forever.

"You danced with that duke," her aunt ground out. "Went out with him on the terrace to do I don't know what horrid thing. And then you were mincing around him in the park two days ago. I know your whore ways."

Adelaide shut her eyes briefly. Opal was always so poised to find fault in her behavior, she was often shocked that her aunt hadn't figured out that she snuck out of the house three times a week to do something far more scandalous than merely dance with a duke.

But Opal looked for other kinds of sin in Adelaide, because of her past. She was blind to anything else, a fact Adelaide had used against her during her time as Lydia. All it took were a few sympathetic servants like her maid and some careful balancing acts when it came to entering and exiting the house.

"I assure you, aunt, Northfield and I are…" She hesitated as she thought of Graham's hands on her. Of his whispered secrets. Of the depth with which she was beginning to care for him. "I'm *nothing* to him," she finished. "Just a wallflower who is a friend to his best friend's wife. He is polite to me, nothing more."

"I know when a man has interest in a woman!" her aunt all but screeched. "I saw him leering at you in the park. And I see that look in your eyes when you talk about him."

Opal came forward in three long steps, and Adelaide braced herself. But she was in no way ready for what her aunt did next. Opal's hand shot out, and suddenly her fingers curled hard around Adelaide's throat.

"Don't play with me, you dirty girl," Opal hissed. Her eyes had gone almost bleary, like she was no longer with Adelaide.

"Don't you dare."

Adelaide clawed at her aunt's hands, sucking for breath as she fought the surprising strength of Opal's grip. And Opal was squeezing, squeezing, almost like she wished to end Adelaide. Her vision began to blur and she slapped at her aunt's hands now, fighting for air and her life.

"Stop!"

Opal released Adelaide as they both turned toward the door. Adelaide bent over, and as her vision cleared she found Emma standing in the entryway, with a shocked and horrified Smith at her side.

"What in the world are you doing?" Emma cried, crossing the room in three long strides and clasping an arm around Adelaide. "Darling, are you all right?"

Adelaide stood, sucking in long breaths. "Y-yes," she stammered as the reality of what had just happened became clear. "Yes, I'm—I'm fine."

Emma looked her up and down, uncertainty clear on her face. Then her expression hardened. Emma became a person Adelaide had never seen before. Long gone was the wallflower Adelaide had called a friend for years. In her place was a duchess, a woman of power. Of confidence. Of fire.

And Emma turned all of that on Opal as she arched one fine brow. "How dare you, madam," she said, her voice cold as ice.

"You come to my home, telling me how to handle *my* ward?" Opal cried, folding her arms. Adelaide could tell, though, that she was tentative in the face of Emma's new strength.

It seemed Emma could see it too, for she lifted her chin. "Adelaide will come join me for supper," Emma declared. "And she will stay with Abernathe and me at our home tonight."

Opal jolted. "No," she said firmly.

Emma moved toward Adelaide's aunt. "I was *not* asking. Adelaide is going with me. *Now*. And I will expect that her maid will be sent after her with her things for a night away. Do I make myself clear?"

Opal swayed slightly, and Adelaide braced herself for a verbal attack. She didn't think her aunt would try anything physical with Emma. She wouldn't dare face off with the power that was Abernathe. Even her aunt would not be so foolish.

"Fine," Opal said at last, her shoulders rolling. "Whatever you'd like."

Then she turned on her heel and stomped from the room without another word. Emma watched her go, then turned her attention on Smith. "Are my instructions clear, Smith?"

"Yes, Your Grace," Smith said with the faintest of smiles for Adelaide. "I'll make sure Rebecca gets everything together and is sent to your home as soon as possible."

"Excellent," Emma said, going back to Adelaide and putting her arm around her again. "Then I will take Adelaide now."

Adelaide stared at her. "Emma…"

"No refusals," Emma said, in almost the same tone she had used with Opal. A tone of strength and confidence. Adelaide found she rather liked it. She envied it.

Only Lydia had that tone. Adelaide had never mastered it when she didn't wear a mask.

So she followed Emma, out of the house, into her carriage. It was only when they were moving that Emma's cool countenance fell and she rushed to Adelaide's side of the vehicle to hug her.

"Oh, Adelaide!" Emma all but sobbed. "What in the world happened?"

Adelaide stared at the floor, humiliation and pain and fear hitting her at last now that she was safe. Tears pricked behind her lids and she had no strength to fight them, so she let them fall.

"It's nothing," she tried to argue, but Emma shook her shoulders gently.

"She was choking you!" Emma cried. "You were turning blue. Please stop lying to me."

Adelaide bent her head. "Very well. She came into the

room, making accusations about my guardianship of my virtue."
She chose her words carefully, since she'd always kept Emma
in the dark about so much. At first because she didn't want
Emma to worry when she was in no better position. Now
because she didn't want to mar her happiness.

"And that inspired her to attack you?" Emma asked.

Adelaide drew in a deep breath. "I didn't expect it," she
whispered. "I was…terrified."

"I can well imagine." Emma held her tightly, and Adelaide
allowed her head to drop to Emma's shoulder. They sat like that
for a while, then Emma sighed. "You will not return."

Adelaide jolted. "Opal would never allow it."

Emma snorted out derisive laughter. "Let her go to battle
with James over that. I would wager he'll win."

"Why would he do that?" Adelaide asked.

Emma blinked as she looked at her. "Because he loves me.
And I love you. Of course he would stand up for what was right."

"I'm getting to be with you two tonight," Adelaide said,
unwilling to argue over what she knew Opal would do. Her aunt
had always jealously guarded her power over Adelaide. She had
no doubt she would fight to keep it, even though she felt no love
for her niece. "That will have to be enough."

Emma shifted and slowly moved back to her side of the
carriage. She met Adelaide's stare. "I must tell you something."

Adelaide wrinkled her brow at the change in Emma's
demeanor. "Very well," she said slowly. "Though your
expression is very ominous."

"Graham will be joining us tonight."

Adelaide shut her eyes slowly. "Of course he will be," she
muttered. It was entirely fitting. A few days ago she had seen
him at his lowest and most vulnerable. Tonight she was at hers.

And he'd be there. And he wouldn't care.

"You sound disappointed," Emma said. "You like him,
don't you?"

Adelaide looked at Emma and her heart sank. Her friend
had never been much able to hide her heart, her hopes. Now they

were written all over her face. She wanted Adelaide to somehow find an impossible match with Graham.

"He doesn't like *me*," Adelaide said slowly, both avoiding her friend's question and trying to gently end her hopes. End her own.

Emma tilted her head. "How do you know that?"

Adelaide almost laughed though there was nothing amusing about the situation. "I just do," she said with a shake of her head. "He wants…something I am most certainly not."

Emma was quiet for a long moment, then she leaned forward. "I was something James didn't want. Or thought he didn't. And here I am."

Adelaide smiled, for in that moment Emma had never been more beautiful. She had a baby growing in her stomach, her face was lit with a love so pure and powerful and true that it almost glowed from within her. She had faith in the world, in her husband, in herself.

And Adelaide had never been so happy for, nor so jealous of a person all at once. With effort, she reached out to take Emma's hand. "I'm not you, love."

Emma caught her breath, and Adelaide could see that she wanted to fight that statement. Deny it. Force Adelaide to become something she knew she could never be.

But there must have been something in Adelaide's face that stopped her. For Emma merely squeezed her hand and allowed Adelaide to collapse back against the carriage seat.

"When will he come?" Adelaide asked.

Emma frowned. "A bit before eight. For supper."

Adelaide nodded. That gave her a few hours to prepare herself for him. For the fact that when he saw her, she would see the man she was starting to care for.

And he would only see the wallflower he tolerated.

CHAPTER THIRTEEN

Graham entered the foyer and handed his hat, coat and gloves to James's butler.

"Their Graces and Lady Adelaide await you in the blue room," the man intoned as he began to walk up the hallway.

Graham nearly tripped over his feet. "Lady Adelaide is here?" he asked.

The butler didn't stop moving. "Yes, Your Grace. She is joining the family for supper." He stopped at the parlor and opened the door. "The Duke of Northfield," he announced, and stepped out of the way.

Graham took a deep breath as his world moved into half-time. Adelaide was in that room. Adelaide, the other half of his present dilemma. The other woman that occupied his mind. That she was here was providence.

Or a devilish coincidence that would only make things harder.

Perhaps both.

He stepped into the room. He knew he should look toward James and Emma, who were standing together before the fire. He didn't. His gaze moved immediately to Adelaide. She had obviously been seated on the settee, but now she stood, her hands clenched before her, her bespectacled gaze focused on him.

She was nothing like what he had pictured when he thought

of a woman who would capture his attention. But she had it. All of it. Even his obsession with Lydia faded when he entered a room with Adelaide in it.

"Good evening," he forced his mouth to say.

"Good evening," Adelaide responded, her voice shaking just a fraction.

Before Graham could analyze that overly much, James and Emma came across the room to greet him. "Hello, mate," James said.

Emma reached for him. "I'm so glad you're here, Graham, we'll be a very happy foursome—my goodness, Graham, your hands!"

Graham glanced down. Without his gloves, his bruised and marred knuckles were very clear. Emma had gone pale as she looked at them, and even James seemed concerned.

When he glanced at Adelaide, he was surprised that she was staring at his face, not his hands. He cleared his throat. "Ah, yes. I, er...well, I suppose I have some news for you two. I don't know if I should say this in front of Lady Adelaide, though."

Adelaide's jaw set slightly and she moved as if to leave the room, but Emma held up a hand. "Adelaide is my dearest friend. You may say whatever you wish in front of her. Come, let us sit."

She motioned for the chairs and the settee in front of the fire. She and James took the chairs, and Graham's heart began to pound. The only place left was the one next to Adelaide. She seemed to notice that fact the same time he did, for her cheeks darkened to a deep pink.

He smiled at the reaction, for it meant she was not as immune to him as she always pretended to be. She sat and he followed, not sitting too close, but close enough that he could feel just the hint of her warmth. Suddenly he felt it keenly. Smelled her soft, fresh scent. And wondered, with a powerful jolt, what it would feel like to touch her lips with his own.

He blinked the thoughts away and refocused.

"Sir Archibald is in London," he said.

Emma's reaction was immediate. She jumped to her feet, all color leaving her cheeks and stood staring at him. James followed, catching her arm to steady her as he, too, kept his gaze on Graham.

"What?" Emma finally burst out. "*Here?*"

Graham nodded. "After what happened in Abernathe in the early summer, I did track him for a while. But the situation with Simon…" He hesitated, looking at Adelaide. Her gaze darted between himself, James and Emma.

"What happened in Abernathe?" she asked.

Emma trembled as James helped her into her seat. "My father made an arrangement for me to marry that bastard," she whispered. "James saved me, but Sir Archibald was enraged. He attacked me and nearly—"

She broke off. James's face was red as he said, "I kept him from hurting her. I should have killed him."

Graham bent his head. "Well, *I* nearly did. You see, he has been lurking about the theatre as of late. He was bothering a…a friend of mine." He shot Adelaide a glance, but she didn't look at him. She almost seemed to be doing it on purpose.

"A friend?" James repeated, his eyebrows lifting.

Graham glared at him. "A friend."

"Was she hurt?" Emma whispered. "The poor woman, was she injured by him?"

It was clear what she meant by injured, and Graham reached out to gently take her hand. She lifted her eyes to his and he said, "No, Emma. I stopped him. I nearly killed him, but my…my friend was wise enough to stop me."

"A good friend, indeed," Adelaide said softly.

He turned his gaze on her. "Yes," he agreed with a sigh. "Honestly, Emma, he fears James. I don't think he'll pursue you. He much prefers women who have no such protection that you do."

The color in Emma's cheeks returned a little with that statement, but James's jaw was set with a barely controlled rage Graham recognized. "I shall employ a guard," he said through clenched teeth.

Graham nodded. "I can help you arrange that."

Emma let out her breath gently. "I suppose it wouldn't hurt to have a few extra men as protection."

Adelaide voice trembled as she said, "Yes, I think it wise, but Emma, why didn't you tell me about Sir Archibald?"

Emma shook her head. "There was so much that happened. And it was a moment of horror in the midst of such happiness. I just didn't want to speak of it."

Adelaide's expression gentled, and there was a wealth of understanding there. Enough that Graham wondered how she could be so empathetic. Had someone hurt her at some point? The idea stoked an anger in him, rivaling what he'd felt when Lydia was attacked. He took a few breaths to calm it.

"Well, we must speak of happier things now," he said. "Unless you have more questions, Emma?"

Emma smiled at him. "You are very kind, Graham, but no. I think you're right that talking the past to death will do us no good. James and I know about Sir Archibald now. And I'm certain, given my husband's protective expression, he will take care of me."

James spun on her. "I will, Emma. I vowed that to you and I meant it."

He shocked Graham by tilting Emma's chin up and pressing a brief but passionate kiss against her lips. Graham turned his head and found Adelaide was also staring at a loose thread on the settee. Her cheeks flamed as she lifted her eyes to him.

In that moment, he wished he were so free as to be able to kiss her. He wondered what she tasted like. What she would feel like in his arms. What her sighs of pleasure would sound like. How she would move her delicate hands across his skin.

"Your Graces," James's butler said from the doorway. The group turned toward him, and he nodded. "Supper is served."

Emma took a long breath and then slid her hand into the crook of James's arm. "Shall we?" she asked as she motioned to the door. They exited, and Graham turned to Adelaide.

Touching her in this moment seemed very dangerous, but there was no avoiding it. He held out his elbow and lifted his brows. "May I take you, Adelaide?"

She caught her breath quietly and her gaze darted away from his. She nodded, but the movement was jerky. "Y-yes," she stammered. "Of course."

She glided toward him, graceful in her movements, and then her fingers folded around his arm. He fought every urge within him to groan at the gentle touch and instead moved toward the dining room.

A place where he hoped he could gather his senses before he lost all ability to control himself.

Adelaide shifted as she felt Graham's gaze turn on her yet again. It felt like the hundredth time this evening, and she hardly knew how to react.

"How did you and Emma meet, Adelaide?" he asked.

She jerked her face up to look at him. He truly seemed interested in the answer, just as he had when he'd asked her a dozen other questions during supper.

Fighting for control over her emotions, she shot Emma a look. "We met at a tea party hosted by…" She trailed off.

"Lady Laura of Liars," Emma finished with a giggle that warmed the room and took the edge off of Adelaide's discomfort.

"Oh, gracious I'd forgotten about that," Adelaide laughed, covering her mouth with her hand.

"What exactly?" James asked, his expression warm with indulgence as he watched his wife. "Whatever it is, my wife's blush tells me it's a wicked joke between you two hellions."

Adelaide shook her head. "Wallflowers cannot be hellions."

Graham snorted out a laugh and she glared at him. He lifted his shoulders without a hint of apology to his face. "I'm sorry, my dear, I've spent too much time with you as of late to believe that. And Emma clearly has a devilish side or she'd never caught the attention of James."

James winked at his wife and Emma's cheeks turned an even deeper red. "Adelaide and I used to come up with silly little names for some of the meaner girls in our acquaintance," Emma explained.

"To be fair to the honor of your wife," Adelaide interrupted, "*I* started it. Lady Laura, I believe she's…she married the Marquis of Hedgebottom, didn't she?"

Emma nodded. "Twenty years her senior. I've heard she's utterly miserable."

Adelaide smiled despite herself. "Couldn't have happened to a nicer girl. At any rate, she tossed a horrid little set down at Emma, and I'd just received one of my own. So I said something nasty about her being Lady Laura of Liars and it set off from there."

"You two little gossips," James said with a shake of his head. "Standing at the wall, looking innocent and sweet as sugar and all along you had depths galore."

"I've never looked sweet as sugar in my life," Adelaide laughed.

"I would disagree with that," Graham said, and his gaze focused once more on her face.

She shifted beneath his unexpected regard. What in the world was happening? He couldn't possibly like her. It was a foolish notion to even think such a thing. What was happening was that she *wanted* him to like her, the real her, and so she was finding meaning in every fleeting glance. Every offhand comment.

It really had to stop or she'd end up with an even more broken heart than was surely coming when she finally revealed the truth to him.

The servants cleared the last of their supper courses and James stood. "Northfield, would you like to join me for a chat? I think you and I have some arrangements to make."

He shot Emma a brief look and Adelaide recognized the fear that flitted over her friend's expression. Fear over Sir Archibald. She felt terrible she'd never even known Emma's relationship to the bastard.

Graham got up, and his gaze flitted to Adelaide once more. "Yes. Perhaps we could join you ladies after?"

Emma smiled. "Of course."

James moved forward and pressed a kiss to Emma's cheek before he helped her to her feet. Then he smiled at Adelaide and the two men left the room.

Once they were gone, Emma sagged slightly and Adelaide moved to steady her. "You look tired," she said as the two walked to another parlor for their own drinks.

Emma nodded. "I am. I'm still feeling sickly in the morning time thanks to the baby, and sometimes it's as if emotions just...*overwhelm* me. Hearing about Sir Archibald..."

She trailed off, and Adelaide helped her to a seat. "Oh Emma, I wish I'd known."

Emma shrugged. "As I said earlier, I've had such happiness since my marriage, I didn't want to speak of it." She sighed. "James and Graham will take care of it, though."

Adelaide pressed her lips together. "Yes, I'm certain they will."

"You two seem to be growing more connected each time I see you," Emma said softly.

Adelaide glanced at her friend. Emma seemed very focused now, the sharpness back in her stare. And once again Adelaide wanted to tell her everything. *Everything.*

Only she couldn't. Not yet. She owed it to Graham to tell him before anyone else. After...well, after she would tell Emma. Carrying all these lies was becoming far too difficult a burden. And if Graham turned on her, as she had to believe he would, she would need Emma more than ever.

She shivered at the thought.

"You know, Emma, I want to talk to you about it," she confessed. "I have so much to say. But like you, I'm exhausted.

Will you let me wait until another day to confess everything you want to know?"

Emma examined her a moment, then she nodded once. "Of course. But I'm here if you need me. I hope you know it."

Adelaide leaned in to buss her cheek. "After today, I could *never* doubt your friendship. Thank you again for getting me out of that house."

Emma pushed from the chair and sighed. "Come, we'll both go up. I'll send word to James that we're both too tired for any more excitement tonight. He'll explain to Graham."

Adelaide inclined her head in agreement, though there was a part of her that was deeply disappointed she wouldn't get to see the man again tonight. A fact that proved she was being foolish when it came to him. She would do well to remember that.

Emma linked her arm though hers as they began to leave the room. "Adelaide," she said quietly.

"Yes, Emma?"

"It will be better in the morning."

Adelaide swallowed. She wasn't certain that Emma was right in this case. Soon enough, a tomorrow would come where she would have to tell the truth to everyone she cared for, including Graham.

When the day came, she was utterly unconvinced that anything would be all right ever again.

CHAPTER FOURTEEN

Graham sipped his drink as he watched James pace his office restlessly, just as he had been for nearly twenty minutes.

"How many do you think I should hire?" James mused.

Graham leaned forward. "Two will be enough," he said. "One for the day, one for the evening, especially if you aren't here. You don't want to smother Emma, or make her a prisoner in her own home."

James relaxed a fraction and slowly sank into a chair across from Graham. "Of course. You're right, I would never want to do that to her. I just…the idea that the bastard is in London makes my stomach turn."

"That's two of us," Graham muttered. "I'm sorry I didn't keep a better eye on the man. Especially considering how he nearly—"

He cut himself off and stared at his bruised hands as memories flooded him. James stopped pacing to stare at him. "You lost control?"

Graham lifted his chin slowly. James didn't ask the question with judgment, but Graham still felt defensive as he jerked out a nod. "I did."

"It's been a long time since you've done that." James folded his arms. "You must like that actress a great deal."

Graham pursed his lips at the knowing expression on his friend's face. "I ought to know better than to tell anyone in our group anything. It all filters back to you, doesn't it?"

"King of the dukes, yes? I must watch over my kingdom as best I can," James said with a brief smile and a shake of his head. "I *do* wonder what it means for Adelaide, though."

Graham stiffened at the mention of her name. "You think I'm being unfair to her?"

"It's clear you like her, too," James said with a shrug of one shoulder. "I know you well enough to know what I see when you two are together. Funny that I couldn't see the trouble between you and Meg so clearly."

Graham ran a hand through his hair, loosening it from its queue in the process. He shook his head. "That wasn't your fault. You did what you thought was right for everyone involved. Any one of us could have stopped it before it…blew our lives apart."

James tilted his head. "Why didn't you? You clearly didn't love Meg any more than she didn't love you. Why didn't *you* stop it?"

"Most of our station don't marry for love," Graham said after a long pause where he considered the question. Considered the two women who were so confusing him. "I never thought I would. In truth, I never thought I'd want to. Strong emotion never…never seemed positive to me."

"Because of your father," James said softly.

Graham flinched despite himself. "Yes. His passions always led to anger. I fear I may follow in his footsteps."

"You never could," James said instantly and firmly as he came forward to clasp a hand on Graham's forearm. "You could *never* be like him."

Graham shut his eyes, thinking once again of Sir Archibald's broken face the previous night. Feeling the thud of flesh on flesh in his sore knuckles even now. His stomach turned.

"You asked if it's fair to Adelaide," he said, forcing the subject change without any finesse. "I know it isn't. I do like her, James, I want you to know I'm not playing a game with her. She isn't like anyone I've ever known before. I find myself wanting to peel away all those layers she puts up between herself and the world. But then there's Lydia, and I've already given her secrets I never even told you or Simon."

James leaned back in surprise. "I see. Do you think there's a future with the actress?"

Graham drew in a long, ragged breath. When he pictured a future, he couldn't conceive of it without Lydia. But then again, he also had a hard time picturing it without Adelaide.

"If you take so long to answer, I can see what you don't want to say," James said. "I don't know Adelaide very well yet, but I know from everything Emma has said that she deserves better than half a heart. If you feel such a deep connection to Lydia, I think you ought to—"

He broke off and Graham shook his head. "Tell me, I want to know."

"I'm afraid you won't like it," James responded slowly.

"Well, Simon isn't here to soften the blow," Graham said with a small smile. "So say it quickly and perhaps it will sting less."

"I think you ought to let Adelaide go," James said firmly.

Graham could hardly breathe at the thought, even though he knew James was right. Even though he only spoke the absolute truth.

"Your Graces?" Both men turned as James's butler entered the billiard room. As James nodded, the man continued, "The Duchess and Lady Adelaide have both decided to retire to bed early. Her Grace says to tell you to stay up as long as you'd like, Your Grace."

Graham sent a side glance at James. From the shift in his expression, Graham could see his friend wanted to join his wife. The certainty on Abernathe's face made Graham's chest tighten. He wished he knew what he desired so clearly.

"Thank you," James said. "You may also finish your duties and go to bed. I'll make sure the doors are locked after Northfield leaves."

The butler nodded and left the two men alone. James smiled

at him. "It seems we have a long night available to us if you'd like to talk."

Graham laughed despite himself. "No, I don't require a governess tonight, though I appreciate the offer. I would like to say one thing before I tell you to go to your bed and let me show myself out."

James nodded. "Of course."

"The situation is untenable, and I know you're right that I shouldn't toy with a woman like Adelaide. Nor a woman like Lydia. Still, they have given me a gift."

"And what is that?"

"I understand more what Simon…went through," he admitted slowly. "Wanting what he felt he couldn't have, loving what he knew he shouldn't. I can see how his desperation could have led him to do something. How he could have been willing to trade anything not to lose Meg."

James's jaw twitched a little. "If that is what you've gotten from your current predicament, then I cannot be sorry. I hope that means one day you can talk to Simon, forgive him even. Our world is not the same without you."

Graham stiffened. "I'm here."

James shook his head. "You're not really. Not the way it used to be. Perhaps that's too much to hope for, but I still do."

Graham nodded. In truth, as time passed, he had begun to wish for how things used to be too. It might not be fully possible with all they'd gone through. But he knew that avoiding the situation wasn't going to change it. "I will speak to Simon when I'm ready, I promise you."

James slapped his arm again. "Can you show yourself out?"

He smiled. "I can. I'm sure Grimble hasn't gone to bed and I can convince him to lock up behind me. I'll talk to you again soon."

James grinned and left the room, Graham trailing behind him. While his friend turned right toward the stairs, Graham maneuvered left, down the long and winding halls that led to the foyer. But as he turned in a bend, he slowed his gait. The library door was open a crack and there was a sliver of light peeking out from the space, leaving a beam in the hallway. He edged toward it, his heart rate increasing because he knew instinctively what he would find in that room.

He also knew he should walk past it.

But he didn't.

Adelaide's bare foot tapped beneath her gown, and she looked up at the shelves of books without seeing any of them. God, how she was distracted. She hadn't even had the focus enough to ring for Rebecca to help her undress. All she could think about was Graham, Graham, *Graham*.

Graham, shame filling his face when Emma noticed the bruising on his knuckles.

Graham watching Adelaide at supper, his expression hooded and unreadable, but oh-so-focused and confusing.

Graham, broken the night after he'd attacked Sir Archibald. Broken as he whispered his dark and painful secrets to a woman who didn't even exist.

And Graham, who was just a few doors down the hall with James, talking about God knew what while she couldn't stop thinking about him.

"Hello, Adelaide."

She froze in her place facing the bookshelf and her heart began to pound so hard she feared it could be heard in the silent room. She'd thought she was safe here tonight. She'd thought Graham and James would likely spend many hours talking together.

It seemed she was wrong. She pivoted slowly and found exactly what she expected: Graham standing at the entrance to the room. His blond hair was half out of its queue and strands of it fell around his face, making him look undone and a little dangerous.

Because of course he was there when she was at her most vulnerable. *Of course* he was there, watching her, when her secrets were so close to the surface. When she knew she'd have to tell him, but just wasn't ready yet.

"Hello," she squeaked out.

He hesitated a moment, almost as if he were weighing his options, and then stepped fully into the library and gently shut the door behind himself.

She stared at him. They were inappropriately alone now. She had never been alone with him like this as Adelaide. Brief moments on the terrace were nothing like this, where the room was so small and tight and no one knew they were here together.

No one could interrupt.

Despite the danger of this moment, despite her foolishness in wishing it would grow more dangerous still, her body reacted of its own accord to what he'd done. She started to tingle, making it very clear what she wanted from the man no more than three feet away from her.

"I thought you'd gone to bed," he said, and she was almost certain he gave the word *bed* just a tiny bit more weight.

She worried her hands in front of herself. "I couldn't sleep. Not that I tried that hard."

He moved a hand up to brush a lock of hair from his forehead and she tracked the motion, drawn once again to the bruises on his knuckles. She should have asked for ice. It would have helped the swelling. He frowned at how she looked at his injuries.

"Ugly, aren't they?" he said, holding his hands out so she could look more closely.

She caught her breath. "I don't think so."

"No?" he pressed, coming forward a step. He brought his body heat with him, his unwavering presence that seemed to take up all the space, all the air, everything she needed to survive.

She should have stepped away, but instead she reached out. Her fingers nearly brushed the bruising, but he pulled back, ducking his head.

"What you must think of me," he said softly. "You and Emma."

She pursed her lips, frustrated that he knew so little of her real self that he would think she'd judge him for what he'd done. Pained that he judged himself even more harshly.

"You did something brave, it seems to me," she said, choosing her words carefully. "To protect your...your *friend* as you did."

He winced. "If you were there, you would have thought me an animal, Adelaide."

She fisted her hands at her sides. "Of course you weren't an animal, Graham," she insisted, her emotion bubbling over even though she didn't want it to. "That man's intentions were clear— he wouldn't have stopped unless you stopped him. What would have happened then? I know exactly what would have happened. I would have been raped and—"

She cut herself off and jerked her hands to her lips. What had she just said? In her fervor to soothe Graham, what in the world had she just said?

Graham lifted his gaze to her and his brow wrinkled with confusion. "What did you say?"

She backed up, and this time he didn't hesitate to move forward. He tilted his head now, examining her. *Really* looking at her.

"I didn't say anything," she said. "I-I was just repeating what you said about your friend."

"You said *I* would have. *I*, not she." He moved closer again and she staggered, almost tripping off the edge of the rug as her backside hit the bookcase behind her. He pressed farther into her space, not quite touching her, but looming up nonetheless, his face too close to hers.

His bright, impossibly blue gaze piercing. And *seeing*. Her breath grew ragged, the only broken sound in the quiet room around them. She wanted to turn and run, but there was nowhere to go. Nowhere to hide. Not anymore.

"Graham," she whispered. "Please don't."

He reached for her and she braced for him to catch her arm. To yell and demand and reveal. Instead, he silently slid his fingers into the tight bun that was bound up at her nape. She went weak at the touch, the feather-light pressure of his hand against her scalp, gliding her pins loose to scatter on the floor below her, spreading her hair out and down across her shoulders.

His nostrils flared.

"Graham," she repeated weakly, tears filling her eyes.

He slid his hand around to her chin, forcing her to look up at him. Then he brushed his fingertips across her jaw, over her cheekbone, and caught her spectacles. Slowly, slowly he glided them down over her nose and away.

And he stared at her. Without her armor, without her costume, without her barriers between them. And he saw her. Because there was nothing left to keep him from doing so.

She stopped breathing entirely, mostly because she couldn't remember how to do so when she was so exposed. This wasn't how she'd wanted him to find out her secret. This moment when he was just *staring* at her, his expression one of coiled emotion.

She braced for him to yell at her. To demand she explain herself. Or worse, to simply walk away in pure disgust.

But instead he let out a long breath and whispered, "Thank God."

Then his mouth was on hers with a crushing desperation that was unlike any way he'd ever kissed her before.

CHAPTER FIFTEEN

If there had been any doubt left in Graham's mind, and there hadn't been, all of it fled the moment his lips touched hers. Adelaide and Lydia were the same person. And he'd never been so confused, so stupefied or so relieved in his entire life. The idea of losing one of the women had been physically painful to him.

Now he knew he wouldn't have to lose either. And he dove into the kiss, tasting Adelaide's desire, feeling it in the way she arched against him with those tiny sounds of pleasure that always rocked him all the way down to his very core.

Reason fled, questions fled, all that remained was this burning desire to have her, to claim her. Not as Lydia, but as Adelaide. As whatever woman she was when she allowed those two sides of her to combine.

He pivoted, backing her toward the settee in the middle of the room. She never resisted as he lowered her onto the cushions, his mouth not leaving hers as he delved deeper and deeper into the ocean that was this woman. Body and soul. He wanted it all. He wanted it now.

She reached up and started tugging at his cravat as his mouth moved away from her lips to her throat. She managed to loosen it and he sat up, shrugging out of his jacket and tearing open the buttons of his shirt until he could tug it over his head.

She lifted her hands to his chest, tracing the lines of muscle there as her eyes went wide. He smiled at the expression, for she'd seen him like this a few times and yet she still seemed shocked every time. It gave a man a swelled head to have a woman look at him like that.

Especially this woman.

He pulled her to a seated position and glided his hand down her spine, flicking open her buttons one by one even as she lifted her mouth back to his with heated, desperate need. They tugged the dress and chemise down together, and he shoved her back on the settee as he latched his lips around one tight nipple. She arched beneath him, her hands coming into his hair as she shut her eyes with a shuddering sigh.

He watched her face as he pleasured her—there was Lydia, there Adelaide. And he tamped down all his questions for the moment.

"Please," she murmured, her hips jolting up against his in time to the way he suckled her breast. "Please."

He nodded and got up, yanking off his boots and fighting with the buttons on his trousers as she shimmied her dress off her hips. She blushed as she slowly opened her legs and revealed herself to him. He stopped what he was doing and stared.

In that moment, she was all Adelaide. And even though he'd had this body before, he'd never known it was her. Now that he did, it was all new again. She was new. And he wanted her with more power and passion than he'd ever desired Lydia.

Which was saying a great deal.

"My God, you are amazing," he muttered as he dropped his trousers, kicked them away and slowly lowered himself over her. "Do you have any idea what you do to me?"

She smiled as she reached between them and gently cupped his rock-hard cock. "I have a little idea."

He shook his head. "Not that. I acknowledge you do that, but I'm not talking about that. I'm talking about this."

He took her hand and lifted it away from his cock, sliding it between their bodies until her fingers rested against his chest, just over his heart. She swallowed hard and met his gaze as he positioned himself against her sex. As he drove forward, his heart rate ratcheted up and her eyes went wide.

She held her hand there, his heart pounding against her palm as he took her with long, slow strokes. Her sex clung to him, squeezing as she lifted against him, her gaze going blurry with pleasure as he took her. He drove deep, circling his hips as she squeezed, and raw sensation rushed up his cock and spread through his entire body. He was alive, he was on fire, and there was nothing like it.

Nothing like her.

He cupped the back of her head, tilting her mouth for better access. He drove his tongue past her lips, tasting her unique flavor as her body began to shake beneath his. He gripped her hip, grinding harder over her, forcing her pleasure until she bucked beneath him, her pussy gripping him as waves of release rolled between them.

She milked his cock, driving him toward home, toward her, toward that blinding moment of perfect pleasure that always existed between them. He thrust harder, shutting his eyes, sucking her tongue, feeling the intense sensation grow until his balls tightened. Biting back his roar, he withdrew, pumping his hand over his cock as he came between them, then flopped forward to cover her body with his as he rained gentle kisses down the slope of her neck and shoulders.

She wrapped her arms around him, cradling his body against hers, her legs tucked around his waist, her soft sounds of pleasure still warm and incoherent against his neck.

And in that moment everything in his world, his life, his riotous mind, was perfect.

That was what she did for him. Adelaide. Lydia. Both. The same. And that thought drew him from the hazy pleasure.

He lifted his head and stared down at her. She was looking straight back at him, not flinching, not hiding. Not anymore. Everything had been laid bare and her secrets would soon merge with the ones he'd confessed so recently.

If she wanted to tell them, that was. Because *she* hadn't

forced *him*. And as much as he wanted to do so, he refused to force her.

He stroked the back of his hand along her cheek, tracing the soft lines there as he whispered, "Tell me?"

She stiffened just a fraction, and her gaze slid away from his. He mourned the connection that had been broken. He mourned that she felt she had to break it. That she couldn't fully trust him. Hadn't trusted him. Might not trust him still.

"I-I owe you that," she said with a nod of what could only be described as resigned surrender.

He cupped her chin and lifted it, forcing her to look at him. Her blue eyes widened, pupils dilating as she met his stare. He shook his head slowly.

"You *owe* me nothing," he whispered. "I'm asking you for the truth, but if you want to protect your secrets I, of all people, would never force them from you."

His answer seemed to shock her, for she was silent for what felt like an eternity. Then she swallowed hard. "No, Graham. I was always going to tell you. And it's time. It's time for the truth."

Adelaide groaned as Graham gently lifted his weight from her. She prepared for him to get up and walk away, to dress, so there would be a barrier between them. But just as he had been from the moment he entered the room, he surprised her. He didn't leave her, but merely shifted them both into a seated position. He tucked her against him, his arms around her, and she rested her head against his bare chest with a shuddering sigh.

She felt safe in his arms. An illusion, she knew, but one she chose to cling to in this moment of vulnerability and fear. He hadn't abandoned her yet, and he already knew the worst of her lies.

"What I told you about the first night we made love when

you thought I was Lydia, it was true," she began, surprised she could make coherent speech when she was shaking so hard. "Three years ago a gentleman began to show interest in me. No one of any real consequence, but he seemed to like me. And no one had ever liked me before. He seduced me. I shouldn't have allowed him to…to take me, but I thought he cared. It seems he didn't, for he disappeared soon after."

She felt Graham's jaw tighten and looked up to see anger on his face. At her? But no, it didn't seem to be. "Who?"

"It doesn't matter now. He ran off to the Americas, his father has said publicly. No one has seen or heard from him in years." She sighed. "He would rather run than marry me, it seemed. At the time, it was devastating, for I knew I'd destroyed any small chance I had at a future. My aunt found out and was enraged, so it made my life at home even harder."

"It changed you," he said softly.

She nodded. "As all experience does, I suppose. I coiled further into myself. Into books. Into the wall. I didn't *want* to be seen."

He looked down into her face and she saw his empathy and understanding slashed across his handsome face. In that moment, her sense of safety grew, despite having told him a fact that could easily change what he thought of her. Lydia's fall was one thing to process. Lady Adelaide's was quite another. Two different worlds, two different feelings on the same subject.

And yet Graham didn't seem fazed by the truth.

"How did it lead you to Lydia?" he pressed gently.

She drew a ragged breath. "I was not happy. As I said, my aunt didn't react well when she discovered I'd been ruined. She would screech the most vile things at me. She would—" She broke off, thinking of Opal's harsh slap during that terrible time. Of the way she'd choked Adelaide just that very day.

"What did she do?" Graham asked, his body stiffening as if he already knew. But perhaps he did, he would know the signs better than most, she would wager.

"She was cruel," Adelaide said softly. "And I was unhappy

and trapped. But she got a head cold a year and a half ago. She was bedridden for almost three weeks, and suddenly I had this tiny taste of freedom again. My maid, Rebecca, who knew how unhappy I was, suggested I sneak out with her and go see a play. It was so wicked, so entirely against character, but I did it."

His eyebrows lifted. "Quite a jump from seeing a play to performing on stage at one of the most popular theatres in London."

She nodded. "It was. You see, Rebecca had a friend backstage, and suddenly we were there. The actress in one of the supporting roles got violently sick and I looked a bit like her. I got pushed out onto the stage with three lines to say and I-I..." She hesitated even as joy flooded her. "I *loved* it. When they applauded, it was like someone had...had turned a light on that I didn't even know existed."

"You are very good, Adelaide," Graham said softly.

She smiled up at him. "Thank you. It snowballed from there. I was asked to do another part and another. Lydia was born, for I certainly couldn't perform as Adelaide. Rebecca and I have an elaborate system for my sneaking out and in. Aunt Opal hasn't suspected...yet."

Graham nodded. "Remarkable. But you must think me a great fool, not to have realized you were Lydia."

"Do you know how many men in our circles came to my plays?" she asked, sitting up and turning to face him fully. "Even came back to talk to me as you did that first night?"

"I assume none of them kissed you," he said, leaning forward to brush his lips back and forth against hers gently. "Nor did they ultimately take you to their bed, as I did."

She shivered as he let his fingers drag down the slope of her neck and across her bare breast before he settled his hand back against his muscular thigh.

"No," she admitted. "None of them did. But I created a character, Graham. Lydia, who possessed all the confidence I lack as Adelaide. She is bold and unafraid. She dresses differently, she moves differently, not to mention that I wear the spectacles and pull my hair back when I'm Adelaide."

"As a shield," he murmured.

"You saw *exactly* what I wished you to see," she said. "Though I admit that first time you approached me to dance after you kissed Lydia at the theatre, I was petrified you had discovered me. And then I was…a little jealous of myself." She shifted. The truths were on the table now, but Graham seemed no angrier to hear them now than he was when he'd realized she and Lydia were the same. That gave her some of the boldness she had created in her character. "May I ask you something?"

He nodded slowly. "You may."

"Why…why did you say thank God when you realized Adelaide and Lydia were the same?" she asked.

He tilted his head. "Don't you know?"

"No, or I wouldn't have asked." She smiled a little.

"*There's* the Adelaide who so easily puts me in my place," he said, a chuckle bubbling from his lips and warming her. "I said thank God because I have been torturing myself for weeks now over you and Lydia."

She wrinkled her brow. "What could you possibly mean?"

"Adelaide, I wanted you both. And I had no idea that you were the same person. Here I was, wrecked by a betrayal from one of my closest friends, and yet I was thrown back and forth between two remarkable women, like a complete bastard."

She stared at him, eyes widening as his statement sank in. "I don't understand. You wanted *Lydia*. Not me."

"I think I just proved that statement very wrong, *Adelaide*," he said, reaching his hand out to pull her a little closer. "I can do it again if you'd like."

"You wanted me because you realized I *was* Lydia," she said, wanting to give in to the desire in his stare but still confused by his statement.

"She who thinks she knows so much really is in the dark," he said. "You couldn't be more wrong. I have spent days and days coming to terms with the fact that I want *you*, Adelaide. I woke up with your name on my lips and your face in my mind.

When I touched Lydia, I felt as though I was betraying *you*. So please trust that I know my own mind. I most definitely want *you*."

Her heart leapt at that statement and the honesty with which it was put. He meant it. He believed it.

"You must see, though, that I'm not her. I'm not confident or bold or—"

"Well, that is pure poppycock," he interrupted. "You have been bold with me many a time in ballrooms and parlors. In fact, I think the real you isn't exactly the woman who hides behind her spectacles *or* the lady who walks the boards. I think you are something between the two. All the best parts of both."

She blinked for sudden tears stung her eyes at his absolute faith in her. A faith she hadn't felt for herself...perhaps ever.

"I was going to tell you," she whispered. "I was going to tell you the truth."

He lifted both eyebrows and actually looked surprised by that confession. "I'm happy to hear it. But why? If I was so blind, why not let me remain so?"

She shivered. "Because you gave me a piece of your soul that night after Sir Archibald attacked me. I couldn't sit by and keep it without allowing you to know the truth." She met his stare and held there even though it was hard. "When you told me about your past, about your father and your mother, it meant so much to me, Graham. Even though I was little jealous of...of myself."

He smiled slightly, though she could see his pain at the reminder of what he'd told her the night before. "It meant a great deal to me, Adelaide, to trust you enough to tell you my past. I'm glad it was you, not just Lydia, who knows it. And it means a great deal to hear your own. I understand only a few people must know of your subterfuge."

She shook her head. "No one but Rebecca," she confessed. "And my driver, too."

His brow wrinkled. "Not Emma?"

"No," she admitted. "I've wanted to tell her so many times,

but before she was married I didn't want to get her in trouble if the truth came out. You know her, she cannot lie—it isn't in her nature."

Graham nodded. "I can see that. But what about Melinda and the others at the theatre?"

Adelaide laughed. "If they knew I was a lady, the daughter of an Earl, they would *never* allow me to work there. The ramifications would be too great, my aunt would make sure of it. Not to mention that there are some there who might try to use that knowledge against me. Blackmail me."

"So you are the only soul in the world that knows my secret, beyond a few servants," he said.

"And you are the only one who knows mine," she finished with a soft smile for him. One he returned instantly.

"And when would you have told me if I hadn't uncovered the truth tonight?" he whispered.

She caught her breath. This was something he hadn't fully thought through yet. She wasn't exactly ready to help him do so, but she couldn't lie to him. She didn't want to.

"I was waiting for…for…" She blushed and he leaned forward.

"It cannot be worse than anything you've already said," he reassured her.

She shifted, suddenly feeling her nakedness keenly. Clenching her fingers in her lap, she took a deep breath and said, "The last time you were with Lydia, you weren't…careful, Graham."

He stared at her a moment, then his eyes went wide, as if he were remembering the last time he'd made love to her before he knew the truth. "Oh God, I was so upset, so distracted that I…I came inside of you."

How she hated the horror in his voice. "For a woman like Lydia, it might not end the world to have an illegitimate child. But I'm not Lydia, not truly. I wanted to come to you after I could safely say there was no baby. I didn't want my telling you the truth to force you into…into some kind of honorable response."

His jaw tightened. "You mean you didn't want me to be forced into marriage with you."

She nodded. "I'd never do that, Graham. The fact was, I *was* ruined before you touched me. As long as there is no baby—which, based on the timeline, there likely won't be—there is no reason for you to throw yourself away on me."

He stared at her, his brow wrinkled. "You think that's what I would see it as?"

"I don't know," she said softly. "But I know after what you've just been through with Meg and Simon, with your past with your parents, the last thing you should have to do is be forced into a life with someone. I'd never do that to you."

He shook his head. "I would *never* accuse you of doing so."

He pushed to his feet as he said the words, and she watched as a wall came down between them. One she hadn't expected after their connection and their honesty. One that stung her far more than it should have, given her lies, given his kindness about those lies.

"I should go," he said, finding his trousers in the mess of clothing on the floor. "Before we're found."

She swallowed past the sudden lump in her throat. Past the disappointment she hadn't earned. Graham had never made promises to Lydia. And even if he said he wanted her as Adelaide, he'd never acted on those impulses until the truth was out.

He owed her nothing. She would ask for nothing.

She pulled her chemise from her dress and tugged it over her head. "I understand."

He was buttoning his shirt as she spoke and turned on her with a strange expression. "I'm not entirely certain that you do," he said. "Emma says you'll be here tomorrow."

She nodded. "She is trying to keep me here as long as my aunt will allow."

"Why?" he asked, once more his body and face on edge.

She hesitated, not wanting to cause him to think on the

horrible past. "She likes having me here," she lied.

He seemed to ponder the answer a moment, but he didn't challenge it. "Well, I'll return tomorrow. We can discuss all this in more detail then, Adelaide. When neither of us is so…distracted."

She nodded, knowing he was right. Recognizing that some distance was what they both needed. He leaned in and kissed her gently, his mouth probing hers until she opened to him and relaxed against him with a shuddering sigh.

He pulled away, his gaze unfocused and filled with the desire she had come to know so well. Then he shook his head. "Good night, Adelaide."

"Good night," she said, watching him go. Then she sagged against the settee.

When she'd pictured telling Graham the truth, she had never allowed herself to hope that he wouldn't hate her. That it wouldn't destroy all the bonds they had built between them. But he'd been wonderful and understanding and everything she had ever wanted.

And even so, she was left unsatisfied, because he had left with so much between them unsaid. And *she* was left with growing feelings in her heart that could only leave her disappointed.

CHAPTER SIXTEEN

If Graham had left Adelaide's side the night before with confusion and emotion clouding his judgment, he returned to Emma and James's house late the next morning with even more of the same. He'd spent an entirely sleepless night thinking of her. Of what she'd told him. Of the fact that she demanded nothing from him.

And yet she inspired him to think of terrifying things. Futures he'd told himself he'd never have. A life he perhaps didn't deserve and that might only end in heartbreak. For her. For him.

The door to the parlor opened and he turned, expecting to see Adelaide and his hosts. Instead, it was only Emma who entered the chamber, her pretty face lit by a welcoming smile. He couldn't help but return it, for his friend's wife was nothing but kind and genuine.

"Graham, I'm so happy to see you again," she said, motioning him back to his seat as she took her own. "The others will join us shortly. James had an unexpected visitor who insisted on being seen, so he sent me ahead to chat with you when Grimble said you were here. Adelaide slept a bit late, she is just finishing readying herself but will join us soon."

Graham swallowed. If Adelaide had slept late, that was likely his fault. After all, he had been the one to keep her up into the wee hours of the morning with passion and secrets.

"I'm sure the two of us will find much to talk about," he said, finding some semblance of politeness even when his mind was spinning.

Emma nodded, but her dark gaze was very focused on him. Like she was reading him. "James told me you once encouraged him to pursue me."

Graham was happy he had not been offered a drink as of yet, or he surely would have spit it across the room at her unexpected statement. He smoothed his hands over his waistcoat and nodded. "I did, Your Grace."

"I'm forever grateful for that," she said, leaning forward. "And so very grateful to see you begin to return to the circle of friends who love you dearly. It means so much to my husband. I do wonder, though…"

She trailed off, and Graham set his jaw. She was direct, but also hedging, questioning herself. "What do you wonder?"

"Adelaide is my friend," she said, her tone still firm despite its softness. "My best friend in the world, one who has seen me through a great deal. I would not wish to see her hurt."

"James spoke to you?" Graham eased out carefully, uncertain whether to be offended or understanding of his friend's loose lips when it came to his bride.

Emma lifted both eyebrows slightly. "No, he didn't. I'm speaking from my own observations, Graham. My own understanding of the situation between you."

He nodded slowly. "Do you think I'm not good enough for her?"

She laughed. "You are one of the most sought-after men in Society. And what matters more is that I know you are a good and decent man. It has nothing to do with your value. Just how much you would value her. If you don't have intentions for a future for Adelaide, I hope you'll consider backing away. Else she'll be hurt and I would hate for that to happen."

"You are a good friend to her," Graham said softly.

"Well, you would know about being a good friend," she replied. "You have always been the best of friends to those you love. And I know you understand where my heart is, for you've been protective of those you care for, as well."

He ducked his head. "I do understand, Emma."

She smiled at his use of her given name, at the understanding it represented. Then she shook her head. "Gracious, I wasn't thinking. Would you like tea?"

She rushed to her feet to pour it, and at that moment the door opened and Adelaide stepped inside. Graham might have answered Emma's question, but he was so taken aback by what he saw that he couldn't.

The woman at the door was not Lydia. But neither was she clothed in her usual costume as Adelaide. She wore a pretty gown, one that didn't contain her clothing's usual high-necked fashion. She didn't wear her spectacles and her hair was done in a looser style, one that framed her face and made her beauty shine through.

She was truly Adelaide now. The woman between her two roles. The woman who had captured him and confused him and made him feel safe enough to confess the darkest parts of himself. And he couldn't stop staring at her in wonder as she blushed prettily and stepped into the room.

Emma followed his gaze, and she, too, caught her breath at Adelaide's appearance. She moved to her. "You are lovely," she said, taking her hand as they stepped toward Graham.

He nodded. "Lovely," he repeated.

Adelaide's cheeks were flaming now, and she ducked her head. "You two will swell my head. It's all Emma's gown, you know. Thank you again for the loan of it."

Emma snorted. "You are welcome, but I assure you, a silly dress is not the cause of your beauty."

Graham smiled in her direction, both for her kindness in the loan and for her compliments of her friend. Adelaide deserved no less.

"Good morning, Graham," Adelaide squeaked out.

His smile broadened. "Good morning yourself, Adelaide."

They stood together for a long moment that seemed to

stretch for an eternity. Then Graham cleared his throat. "Emma, I wonder if I might have a moment alone with Adelaide?"

Emma's lips parted slightly, and she looked at her friend. Graham was happy when Adelaide gave a slight nod, indicating she wanted the same thing he did. Still, Emma shifted her weight.

"Er, I…I really shouldn't leave you unchaperoned," she murmured, glancing from the couple to the door and back again.

Graham arched a brow at her. "But you will. Because you are a good woman."

Emma shot him a look and then nodded. "Very well. I should check on James and his guest, at any rate. See if he needs saving. But I'm leaving the door open a crack, you two. And I will be back *very* shortly."

"Yes, Mother," Adelaide teased as Emma slipped from the room.

The moment she had gone, Graham reached for Adelaide and she stepped into his arms, tilting her face toward his with a shuddering sigh that seemed to sink into his very soul. His mouth covered hers and she opened to him, her body molding against his as he kissed her as thoroughly as he could without coming undone and losing control with her.

As much as he wanted to, it was clear they had no time. When they'd stood in each other's arms for what felt like forever, she broke the kiss and stepped back, her cheeks still flaming like an innocent.

"*That* is a good way to start a morning," Adelaide said with a nervous smile.

"I agree," he said, taking her hand and leading her to the settee where they sat far too close together. He brushed an errant curl away from her forehead and smiled. "I like this look on you, Adelaide."

She bent her head. "Rebecca was more than happy to help me abandon my severe hair."

"I never asked you, can you see without your spectacles?"

She laughed then, a musical sound that made his heart

lighter. "Gracious, yes. They were only ever for reading, and a slight adjustment at that. I see better without them, truth be told."

He smiled, but then he sobered. There was one question that had plagued him all night, all morning. "Are you sorry about last night?"

Her expression softened as she stared at him, her eyes wide and her lips slightly parted. "Graham, surely you must know the answer to that question."

He shook his head.

She took both his hands in hers and leaned closer. "I have never regretted any moment with you, Graham. Not a one. If I have not made it clear, then I must tell you that you...you brought me back to life. I could *never* regret that."

He caught his breath, for what she'd said was exactly how he, himself, felt but had never allowed himself to examine too closely. Since the end of his engagement to Meg—hell, even before that—he'd felt trapped. Dead inside. Empty.

But the moment he met Lydia, the moment he danced with Adelaide, all that had begun to change. The ice around him that held him in place, kept him cold and broken, had melted with every look and laugh and heated touch.

And calling that being brought back to life was the most apt description he could imagine. He stroked his thumb over her lower lip, ready to tell her he felt the same, but before he could, the door behind them slammed open.

Both jumped to their feet, pivoting to face the intruder. Adelaide swung slightly and Graham caught her elbow to steady her as her aunt Opal stomped into the room with Emma hot on her heels.

"You have *no* right to barge into my home!" Emma snapped out, sending an apologetic look to Graham and Adelaide.

Lady Opal glared at Emma. "You speak of your rights when you all but stole my charge out from under me? When you have left her alone with this...this...animal, who likely smells the whore on her?"

Adelaide flinched and Graham took a long step toward her.

"Have a care with how you speak to the Duchess of Abernathe and to Adelaide, Lady Opal."

The older woman's eyes narrowed and her lined face grew lively with what he could only describe as...*rage*. He knew that rage. He'd seen it many times on his father's own face. He'd felt it that night when he attacked Sir Archibald. On the morning when he realized Simon had betrayed him.

It was out of control. It was violent. And it was turned on Adelaide. In that moment he wanted to tug her behind him, to cocoon her into his arms and protect her from all the vile words this nasty woman had spewed over the years.

But Adelaide didn't ask him to do so. She lifted her chin and stepped around the settee to her aunt with all the bravery of a soldier about to enter into battle. "What are you doing here, Aunt Opal?" she asked, the slight tremor to her voice the only indication of her fear.

"Look at you, with your dress cut down to your breasts and your hair loose like a lightskirt," Lady Opal growled. "*This* is why I don't let you spend the night away."

Adelaide drew in a long breath, ragged and tired, like this was something she'd faced before. Faced so many times. He supposed it was, based upon the secrets Adelaide had whispered to him the night before. His heart hurt for her.

"Why are you here?" she repeated, gentling her tone even in the face of her guardian's cruelty.

"To bring you home," Lady Opal said. "You *need* to come home, Adelaide."

Graham tilted his head at the almost desperate tinge to the woman's tone. She was cruel, but there was something else there. Fear. Anxiety. The sound of it mixed together made the hairs on the back of his neck stand up. There was something irrational to this woman's behavior.

Something that frightened him.

"Adelaide," he said softly. "You don't have to do anything she says."

Adelaide shot him a look over her shoulder. A fearful look,

one filled with uncertainty.

"Aunt Opal," she began, but before she could say anything more James strode through the parlor door with a man Graham didn't recognize at his heels.

"As I said to you three times, inspector," James was saying. "The Duke of Northfield is here and I'm certain he could tell you more about his whereabouts if he wishes to share them."

Graham wrinkled his brow and James did the same as he looked from Adelaide to Opal to Emma and finally to him.

"It seems I've interrupted something in my own house," James said. "Anyone care to explain what's going on here?"

"Lady Opal has come to collect Adelaide," Graham said, lifting his eyebrows in what he hoped was a message James would receive.

If his friend's dark frown was any indication, he did. He turned on Opal. "Adelaide will stay with us, my lady. My wife finds she enjoys her company. It is not up for debate."

Emma smiled as she took her husband's arm and the two faced off with Lady Opal, who was now turning purple. "You have *no* right!" Opal spat.

"I'm sorry to interrupt," the stranger who had accompanied James said with a confused expression. "But I am here on official business."

"And just who are you?" Graham asked, happy to ignore Opal for the moment, even as he kept a careful eye on Adelaide. She looked terrified as her gaze darted from her guardian to her friends to him and then to this stranger in their midst. "I feel I have a right to know if you were asking Abernathe after me."

"Captain Richard Black," the man said with a glance up and down Graham's form. "Of the Home Office."

Graham shot James another look, this one full of questions. "The Home Office? And you were looking for me?"

"For answers," the man corrected with an unpleasant sneer. "I'm investigating an incident that occurred at the Hampshire Theatre two nights ago."

Graham heard Adelaide's sharp intake of breath, but very

carefully did not look in her direction. He kept his gaze firmly on the man before him. He didn't like this Captain Black. He had a smarmy feel to him that told Graham he more than enjoyed his job, especially when he got to take a man down a peg or two.

"An incident?" Graham said mildly.

"With Sir Archibald," Captain Black said with another smile.

Graham gripped his bruised hands at his sides. "I assume you mean the altercation I had when the man attempted to assault an actress?"

"Exactly," Captain Black drawled.

"You see!" Lady Opal cried, launching herself toward Adelaide, hands outstretched. Adelaide staggered back, dodging her aunt's grip as Graham lunged to put himself between them once more. Opal hardly seemed to notice. "You align yourself with the kind of man who would accost a gentleman, Adelaide? You align yourself with a beast?"

Adelaide turned her face, her cheeks red. "Please, Aunt Opal, you must stop."

"I *did* hit the man," Graham said. "I don't deny it, though I'm shocked that he would report such a thing to the authorities."

Actually, he wasn't shocked. He could well picture Sir Archibald would take great pleasure in turning to the Home Office to make Graham look bad after he'd been bested.

"He didn't exactly report the attack," Captain Black said, folding his arms. "Where did you go after the incident?"

Once again, Graham saw Adelaide stiffen from the corner of his eye. Her hands were shaking and she shoved them behind her back.

"I went home," he said softly.

"Home. Were there witnesses to that?" Captain Black pressed.

Graham arched a brow. "My servants will attest to my whereabouts if my word as a gentleman pulls no weight with you, *sir*."

"The word of your servants," Captain Black said with a

shake of his head. "That rarely holds up in court given the influence you hold over them."

"I beg your pardon," James interjected, coming forward. "Are you implying that the Duke of Northfield is lying to you? He's admitted he and Sir Archibald had an altercation—why would he lie about where he went afterward?"

"Because Sir Archibald is dead," Captain Black said, keeping his gaze firmly on Graham. "Shot through the head and found washed up on the riverbank just a short way from the theatre where the duke attacked him. And *you*, Northfield, are the prime suspect in his murder."

CHAPTER SEVENTEEN

Adelaide's ears rang as she watched the room erupt around her in what felt like half-time. Graham was yelling. Captain Black was too, pointing at him. James and Emma moved forward in unison, inserting themselves into the fray. And all the while she could hear her aunt's voice faintly screeching, "He's a murderer, Adelaide! You cannot put yourself in league with a murderer!"

She flinched as those words pierced her very soul. She knew perfectly well that Graham had not killed Sir Archibald. The night of their fight he'd been with her, last night as well. And even if he hadn't, she knew his heart. He was not the kind of man who would kill, even if he had lost control in the face of Sir Archibald's abuse of her.

But the captain was smug and she could see that he was taking great pleasure in accusing Graham. If he chose to pursue this matter, as he was threatening, there was the chance that Graham, this beautiful, wonderful man—this man she loved, for she did love him—would be transported. Or hanged.

"Just tell me that you have an alibi better than servants you pay and I will retract my statement," Captain Black said.

Adelaide swallowed hard and stepped forward. Her hands were shaking as she said, "Stop."

No one heard her. The room continued in its cacophony. She put her hands on her hips and shouted it this time. "Everyone please stop!"

The voices slowed and suddenly five pairs of eyes turned on her. She only looked back at Graham. She looked into those blue depths and her heart swelled with the feelings she had only just admitted to herself and was not brave enough to say to him.

But she would protect him. By God, she would do that.

"The Duke of Northfield could not have killed Sir Archibald," she said softly.

Captain Black tilted his head. "And who are you, miss?"

She cleared her throat. "My name is Lady Adelaide, I am the daughter of the late Earl of Longford."

The captain's face twitched, as if he were just as disgusted by her as he was by the others in the room with titles. "And how do *you* know that Northfield couldn't have killed Sir Archibald?"

She looked at Graham again and his eyes went wide, like he could read her intentions, her heart. She supposed he could, since he owned it. He had since the moment he intruded upon her dressing room weeks ago.

She just hadn't been brave enough to face it until this moment where he was being threatened.

"Adelaide," he whispered, his voice breaking. "You mustn't."

She ignored him. "The Duke of Northfield could not have killed Sir Archibald because he has spent the last two nights with...with me."

Her cheeks flamed as Emma gasped, as James flushed, as Graham dipped his head. As the captain stared at her. She wanted to turn away from their judgments and censure, but she didn't. She couldn't. She had to continue to make sure Graham was fully protected.

"Two nights ago I snuck from my aunt's house to be with him." She swallowed in the hopes her voice would stop shaking. "And last night he came to me here after everyone went to bed. I assure you, Captain Black, that if I am asked to testify to that fact, I will. And I expect I will be believed, given what a mark it will put on my reputation to admit what I've done."

The room was stone silent for one breath, two. And then her aunt let out a scream of rage and agony, and lunged at Adelaide with both her hands raised in attack.

Graham jumped in front of Adelaide as James grabbed for Lady Opal, holding her back by both arms as she spat and screeched unintelligible words of anger.

"Get her out!" Graham bellowed. "Do something worthwhile, man, and help him!"

He said the second to Captain Black, who shook off what appeared to be shock and then stepped forward to help James with the struggling Lady Opal. They dragged her to the foyer and Emma rushed forward to thrust the door shut behind them. She leaned against it, pale as she stared at Graham and Adelaide.

"Are you all right?" she asked.

Adelaide rushed around Graham and wrapped her arms around Emma. "I'm so sorry," he heard her sobbing into Emma's shoulder. "I'm so sorry for the trouble I've brought to your house."

Emma shot Graham a pointed look and guided Adelaide to the settee where they sat together. "Dearest, you are no trouble, this is not your fault. But that woman is dangerous. After this, after what I saw yesterday—"

Graham came to the other side of Adelaide on the settee. "What happened yesterday?"

Adelaide shook her head. "Nothing. My aunt is…she is not well. It's clear."

Emma let out a long breath, and all three turned as James reentered the room. His face was drawn and pale, and he moved to Emma to embrace her.

"Are you harmed?" he asked, his gaze only for her as he settled a hand on her swollen belly.

"No," Emma reassured him before she leaned up for a brief kiss. "We are fine. What in the world did you do with Opal? And with that horrid man?"

He sighed as he sank into a chair, pulling Emma to sit on his knee as he smoothed his fingers over her belly over and over. "Opal calmed the moment we were out the door. She even apologized for her outburst, but dear God, Adelaide, why didn't you tell us how terrible things had become?"

Adelaide let out a shaking sigh that tore through Graham's heart. He took her hand silently and held it with both of his. She glanced at him once, then said, "She normally isn't so wild. But my...virtue, or lack thereof, is an issue for her."

Emma pursed her lips. "Is it true then? That you and Graham have engaged in an affair?"

Graham inched closer to Adelaide, once again driven to protect her in some way. From harm, from censure, from anything that could hurt her.

"Yes," he admitted softly.

Adelaide turned toward him, and he saw the worry in her eyes. "Graham, if Sir Archibald is dead, murdered near the theatre, we must—"

He held up a hand. "*We* must do nothing, I'll go and investigate."

She lifted both eyebrows. "That will not work and you know it. I'm coming with you. I'm not asking."

Graham almost smiled despite the terrible circumstances they had all just endured. By God, but this woman tested him. And he found he liked that. He needed it. He ached for it.

More than that, he needed the protection she had offered. Adelaide had thrown herself in front of him to keep him from being arrested for a murder he hadn't committed. She had done it with what was an obvious knowledge of what her confession could do to her future and her reputation.

And she hadn't cared.

No one had protected him like that since the mother who had died for him. His heart swelled at that thought. At the woman before him.

"Do either of you wish to explain what you're talking about?" Emma asked softly.

Adelaide jumped as if she had forgotten about the presence of James and Emma. She faced them with a blush. "I know I keep saying this, but I *will* explain everything to you, Emma. I promise you I will. Right now, though, I must go with Graham. We have to find out the truth about what happened to Sir Archibald."

Emma opened her mouth as if to argue, but James settled a gentle hand on her knee. "We have very little space to talk about propriety, don't we? Graham will keep Adelaide safe wherever they must go."

Emma blushed as she glanced down at her husband. Then she threw up her hands. "Since I have no idea what is actually going on right now, I feel I have no space to argue. If you must go with Graham, I certainly won't stop you. But I do hope you'll let me in on all these secrets."

Adelaide and Graham rose, as did James and Emma. Adelaide moved to the duchess for a brief embrace. "I will," she promised softly. "And your husband should take you up to bed in the meantime. There has been far too much excitement for a pregnant lady. I want you and that child to be safe."

"Oh, posh," Emma began. "I don't need to—"

"She's going to bed the moment you two leave," James interrupted with a playfully stern look for Emma. Adelaide smiled as she and Emma led the way to the foyer. But as soon as they were out of earshot, James leaned into Graham. "Do you need help? I can come. I can wrangle up three or four of the others to assist, as well."

Graham smiled at James, the best friend he had ever had. The one he'd almost lost. He couldn't help but think of the one he had. And wish that Simon were here, too, to offer support. Kindness.

"We'll be fine," he replied. "I don't think we'll be in danger where we're going."

"And what of Adelaide?" James asked softly. "She made a great sacrifice for you today."

Graham felt the breath go out of him with that statement. The truth of it curled through him once more. "I know," he said as they entered the foyer. "Don't think I don't know. And as soon as this other matter is attended to, I promise you I'm going to deal with that."

His carriage was brought around, and he sighed as he offered Adelaide an arm and guided her to the rig. He would *have* to attend to the things she had said, the way she had protected him to her own detriment. But for now all he could think of was to keep her safe.

He gave a direction to his driver and then climbed in across from her. He shot James a look out the window, and then they were moving and he returned all his focus to Adelaide.

"She has hit you before," he said, not asking.

Adelaide stiffened. "Yes," she admitted softly.

He turned his face as anger flooded him at that thought. "How often?"

She shifted in her seat, her gaze refusing to turn on him. Her cheeks flaming, as if she were embarrassed when she had nothing to be ashamed about. Her guardian was another story.

"She slapped me once, when she found out I'd given myself to a man," she said. "As I said in the house, my virtue has always been an obsession to her. And..." She hesitated, and finally her blue gaze moved toward him. "She put her hands around my throat yesterday morning because she believes I've been lying to her, which of course I have."

Graham stared. "She put her hands around your throat?" he repeated, shocked and horrified.

She nodded. "Emma interrupted, and that's why I came to their home yesterday."

"You *can't* go back to that woman, Adelaide," Graham said through clenched teeth.

She shut her eyes briefly. "Legally she is my guardian, Graham. And in the fourteen years I've lived with her, those are the only two times when she's lashed out at me."

"It escalates," he said through clenched teeth. "A slap. A punch. A choke. A burn. And then he's murdering your mother in the east parlor."

Adelaide's eyes filled with tears and she slid across the carriage to him, touching his cheek and smoothing her thumb across his jawline. "I'm so sorry, Graham. And I know you want to protect me. But I promise you that my situation is not like your own."

He frowned, for he wasn't as certain about that fact as she was. "Adelaide," he began.

She shook her head. "Right now you and I must focus on the situation with Sir Archibald."

"I didn't kill him," Graham said.

She drew back, shock flooding her features. "Of course you didn't," she gasped. "I never believed you did. Even if we hadn't been together the last two nights, I wouldn't have believed it."

"Even after my losing control?" he pressed.

She leaned up and brushed her lips to his. "I *know* you."

It was a simple statement, but it hit Graham straight in the gut. She knew him. Yes, she did. Despite the short time of their acquaintance, she had wound her way inside of him, she had inspired him to whisper secrets he'd vowed never to tell. She had become a part of him.

And he found he didn't want to lose that part, no matter how terrifying a thought that was.

He pushed it aside and sighed. "Either way, I think we both believe his murder is associated with the theatre."

"If his body was found so close by, I cannot imagine it is a coincidence. He had plenty of enemies there."

"Whoever killed that man should be given a medal, not transported," Graham said, sliding an arm around her and tucking her into his side.

She nodded. "Yes, I tend to agree. But the world isn't always fair."

"No," he agreed softly. "It isn't."

The carriage turned a few times as they sat there quietly together, and then it began to slow. He felt Adelaide shift against him, watched her sit up straight, and when he looked at her face, he was shocked to see Lydia there. There was a hardness to her expression, a wariness. He'd never recognized that before when he thought they were two different women. But Lydia was…jaded.

And he found he wanted the real Adelaide back. As much as he'd given to Lydia, as much as he'd needed her in the beginning, now it was different. Lydia represented all the pain that Adelaide sought to escape. Her presence here now only broke his heart.

When the footman opened the carriage door, he climbed down first and helped her do the same. As the vehicle pulled away so it would no longer block the street, Adelaide took a long breath.

"I'm Lydia—don't forget," she said as they made their way toward the theatre.

"Of course."

Her expression changed for a fraction of a moment, as if she was fighting to keep the mask on. But then she was serene again, focused, as they moved around the side of the theatre to a small door he'd never known was there.

"Actor entrance," she explained as they stepped into the cool darkness.

It took a moment for his eyes to adjust as she closed the door and left them in dusty, filtered darkness. During the day the building was quiet, with none of the bustle or noise of a night of a performance.

"Is anyone here?" Graham asked, whispering like they were in a church or on other hallowed ground.

She nodded. "Yes, there's always someone hard at work here. Actors rehearsing, stage people working on props or other set dressing. There's a world of effort that goes into entertaining the *ton*, Your Grace."

She guided him through back hallways that he'd never seen

during his times visiting her here, and finally they popped up behind the stage. A lady stood in the middle of the stage, a seamstress adjusting her hem as she read over lines, testing out different ways to say the same words as she called them out to the empty seats before her.

"Katie?" Adelaide called out, and the actress turned her head. When she saw Adelaide her eyes went wide.

"Good Lord, Lydia! Melinda has been worried sick." Her gaze moved to Graham, curious, wary, and he inclined his head slightly as a greeting.

"Have you heard about Sir Archibald?" Adelaide asked, her tone carefully neutral.

The actress flinched. "Aye, it's all the talk. After what he did to you, to Melinda, and to some of the others, I can't say anyone's sorry for that bastard's demise."

Adelaide's lips pursed. "Yes, there were plenty just within our walls who might want to see him dead. Does anyone know what happened?"

Katie's cheeks paled slightly, and the way her gaze darted away made Graham think she *did* know more. But with him standing there, she clearly had no intention of saying anything.

Adelaide sighed. "Is Melinda here? Or Toby?"

Katie motioned off stage. "Back in your dressing room."

Adelaide reached back and took Graham's hand. "Thank you!" she called out as she guided him down another hallway, the familiar one he'd traveled when he came to call on Lydia after her shows.

"She didn't want to speak in front of me," he said.

She nodded without looking back at him. "For many of these women, a title just means a rich man who does as he likes. Not safe."

He shook his head. "Life for a woman is so very dangerous."

She stopped before her dressing room door and turned to him, smiling. "Yes. Most men don't recognize that, but it's true. And the less power a woman has, the more dangerous it becomes. We have very few laws to protect us, so we must depend on men to do what is right." She reached up and touched his cheek. "Thankfully, some do."

"Not enough," he said softly.

She leaned up to kiss him briefly, then set her shoulders back and opened the dressing room door. As they entered, Graham caught his breath. Adelaide's understudy Melinda was seated on a settee along the wall with a young man who had shown Graham back to Lydia a few times. Toby, he assumed, based on Adelaide's earlier conversations. Melinda's pretty face was battered, both eyes blackened and her cheeks swollen.

Adelaide made a sound of horror and released his hand, rushing into the room as Melinda stood, silent tears streaming down her face while the two women embraced.

"Oh, Lydia," Melinda sobbed. "I was so worried about you."

"I'm fine," Adelaide soothed her as Toby stepped aside and let the two women sit together on the couch. Graham noticed the man watching him warily.

He supposed he'd earned that after the last time he was here and his behavior. All those who worked here must suspect he murdered Sir Archibald, just as the captain had. If he were in their position, he would, too.

"What in the world happened to your face, Melinda?" Adelaide asked, tilting her friend's head gently to look at the damage in better light.

Melinda shot Graham a look, and he frowned. Here was more proof that men of his kind were a threat to women like this. That they lived in fear until they knew a man wouldn't use his power over them.

Adelaide followed Melinda's stare and smiled briefly at Graham. "His Grace is a friend, my dear. I promise you he is not here to do any harm, but to help. You may speak in front of him."

Melinda didn't look entirely certain of that fact, but she swallowed hard and her gaze flitted to Toby. "If Lydia says he's safe," Toby said softly.

"Very well." Melinda took a deep, shaky breath. "After you and His Grace left here two nights ago, Sir Archibald was escorted back to his carriage and sent on his way. But he…but he didn't go home."

Graham clenched his hands behind his back. He could already see the trail of this story. He already knew the end.

"He came back," he offered when the young woman seemed to struggle with the telling.

Fresh tears filling Melinda's blackened eyes. "Yes," she whispered. "He snuck in and he found me. He…he…"

She ducked her head, and Adelaide caught her breath. "He did this to you?"

Melinda nodded slowly, and it was Toby who stepped forward. The young man was slender and wore spectacles and didn't look like much at first glance, but now Graham recognized a deep protectiveness in his stare. And a deep love as his gaze fell on Melinda.

"He did that and more," Toby snarled out, pain making his voice sharp. "When I came in he was—"

He cut himself off and turned away, his shoulders shaking with rage and heartbreak. Graham couldn't help it—he reached out and placed a hand on the man's shoulder as comfort.

"You couldn't have known, Toby," Melinda gasped out. "If you had you would have come sooner. You would have prevented—"

"But I didn't, did I?" Toby asked, turning back.

Adelaide shook her head. "I'm so sorry, Melinda. I'm so sorry that it happened to you. But what happened next? Because the man was found floating in the river just beyond the theatre with a bullet between his eyes."

A heavy silence hung in the room then, a silence that seemed to last forever. Finally, Toby lifted his chin and said, "*I* shot him. I killed Sir Archibald. And I'm not bloody sorry about it."

CHAPTER EIGHTEEN

Adelaide rose to her feet slowly, staring from Toby to Melinda and to the twisted, horrified face of Graham. Pain and empathy flooded her, for what her friend had endured. For what *both* her friends had endured, for she could see that murdering a man, even if justified, weighed on the kind and gentle Toby.

"My God," she whispered. "Oh Melinda, oh Toby. I'm so very sorry."

"I'm not," Toby repeated, just as strong as the first time he'd said it. "I'm only sorry I didn't do it before he touched her."

Melinda rose then and rushed to him, wrapping her arms around him as they trembled together. "It's not your fault. It's not."

Adelaide's eyes went wide as she realized she wasn't seeing two friends who comforted each other. She was seeing two people who were in love and had gone through almost the worst thing imaginable. They leaned against each other, giving comfort and taking strength. She couldn't help but look at Graham in that moment and wish she were so free as to do the same.

But they had not spoken of feelings. Or anything else to do with whatever their relationship had become in the past few weeks.

"We've been hiding here for two days," Melinda explained as she broke away from Toby's arms. "When the Home Office captain comes to question us, as he has a handful of times, the others put us where we can't be found. But we both know it won't last. They'll figure out what happened eventually and then...then..." She bent her head and began to sob softly.

Toby lifted his chin. "I've told you, Melinda, I won't let them know your part in hiding the body. I'll happily be hanged or transported."

Melinda glared at him. This was obviously an argument they'd had more than once. "As if I'd let you take the blame alone. We will go down together."

Graham had been mostly silent since entering the room, allowing Adelaide to manage the exchange, but now he straightened his shoulders and his presence filled the room just as it always did when he chose to allow it.

"I will not let that happen," he said. "I will put all my power behind stopping it."

Toby and Melinda both stared at him, confusion and disbelief in their mutual stares. "Why would you do that?" Toby asked.

Graham hesitated and then said, "Because I understand the drive to protect a woman you...you..." His gaze flitted to Adelaide. "A woman you care about."

Adelaide took in an unsteady breath. Care about? It wasn't exactly a grand declaration of love, not that she had expected one. Caring for her was perhaps the best she would ever get. And yet it felt hollow.

"Besides," he continued, oblivious to her thoughts. "I was asked to watch Sir Archibald months ago, for the very kind of bad acts that he perpetrated upon you, Miss Melinda. I was...I was *distracted* from that duty. If I had not been, perhaps I could have prevented this. Or if I hadn't attacked him the night he moved on Ade—*Lydia* he would not have returned and vented his rage on you. Whatever the answer, I see it as my duty to see that you don't pay for a crime that was my fault."

Melinda stared at him, then to Adelaide. "He would truly do this for us?"

Adelaide nodded, her gaze firmly on Graham. "He would, for he is the best of men."

Graham paced the small room. "I'll arrange for a carriage to pick you up and you'll be taken to a small estate I own just outside London. It will be as good a place to hide as any while I contact a solicitor and we come up with the best plan of attack."

"Could we be married at your estate?" Toby asked, his gaze flitting to Melinda.

Her lips parted, as did Adelaide's. "Marry me, Toby?" Melinda whispered. "Can you mean that?"

He faced her and pushed up his spectacles nervously. "I love you, Melinda. I always have. If we are to be destroyed, I would like a few moments of happiness before it happens. If you'll have me."

She nodded without hesitation, tears flooding her eyes again, though this time they were happy ones. "I will, of course. I do love you, Toby."

She reached out a hand and he caught it, drawing her against his chest. Graham shifted, as if this display of emotion made him uncomfortable. He didn't look at Adelaide as he said, "A marriage could very well make a defense easier. I'd be happy to arrange a special license and have the duty performed at the chapel on my estate."

Adelaide smiled at her friends, happy in this moment, despite the horrors they had so recently endured. She'd known them both for months and had no idea of their feelings for each other. Yet there they were, so clear and so real on both their faces. She felt foolish for not seeing them before.

"You are too kind," Melinda said, breaking from Toby's embrace and reaching out to hold out a hand to Graham. He took it with a gentle smile.

"I don't think you should suffer any more than you have, my dear," he said softly. "If I can prevent it, I shall do anything in my power to do so. Now, if there are arrangements to be made on your side, I suggest you make them. I'll send a carriage for you to the theatre in an hour."

Toby moved forward, his hand outstretched, and the two men shook. In that moment, they were equals. Men who would protect those they loved. Then Toby looked at Melinda. "There are a few things to gather in my office."

She nodded. "Yes, I'll come help you." She faced Adelaide and her lips trembled. "You have been such a friend to me, Lydia. I cannot find the words to thank you."

Adelaide held back a sob as best she could. "It is I who should thank you. You helped me when I was a green beginner, terrified of the stage and of myself. I couldn't have become...*me* without you."

"I hope—I hope we'll see each other again."

Adelaide embraced her gently. "We will, Melinda. We *will* see each other again."

She watched as the two left the room, leaving her alone with Graham. When they shut the door behind them, she moved into the arms he opened for her. He held her like that for a moment, his hands smoothing over her hair as she struggled to come to grips over what had happened.

Then she stepped back. "You were kind to offer them help," she whispered.

He shrugged, like he hadn't just offered two drowning people a lifeline. "We all know Sir Archibald deserved what he got. If I can help them, I will."

Adelaide pursed her lips, looking around the room. She had loved coming here as an escape to the empty life she'd been leading with her aunt. Putting on the costume of Lydia Ford had made her feel confident and powerful and free. But now being Adelaide didn't seem so terrible.

Because of Graham.

And in that moment, a plan began to hatch in her mind. A plan that could save her friends even more than any solicitor or powerful ally Graham could create for them.

She smiled and then took his arm. "Come, we should go back to Emma and James's home. I know they'll be worried."

Graham took a long breath and looked around the room

with her. "This was the first place I kissed you," he said.

She nodded, all the memories of that first night flooding back. "It was."

He turned her toward him and bent his head, brushing his lips to hers. She lifted her hands to his forearms and clung there, not swept away as she had been that first night, but anchored. Anchored by his strength and by her love for him.

And even though she knew she might lose that and soon, she still clung to it in that moment and prayed that somehow she would find the strength to go on, no matter what happened.

Graham had been almost entirely silent as they rode in the carriage, but he sat across the way from Adelaide, just watching her. She couldn't read what was in his mind, but she shifted under the weight of his very focused regard.

At last he cleared his throat and he said, "Your friends are not the only ones to marry soon. You and I will have to do the same, Adelaide."

She caught her breath as she stared at him in shock. "What?"

He tilted his head. "Come, you know it's true. You confessed our affair not only to our friends and your aunt, but to Captain Black. The man has a vendetta against those with a title, anyone can see that just looking at him. He may not pursue me for the murder again, but I wouldn't put it past him to let the truth of our relationship out."

"That isn't why I said what I said," she protested. "I wasn't trying to trap you, Graham. I would never do that."

"Yes, you've made that clear," he said, his voice still soft and even. "By not wanting to confess your double life until you could tell me for certain there was no child created by my imprudence. By never asking me for a damned thing, not as Adelaide or as Lydia. By throwing yourself onto a fire without ever demanding protection in return. There are many things I feel right now, Adelaide, but I *don't* feel like this is a trap."

He let out a long sigh, and she felt his exhaustion and his surrender. Not things she ever wanted from a man in the midst of a rather unromantic proposal.

"If not a trap, then what is it?" she asked, folding her arms as a shield against his indifference.

He met her gaze. "When James arranged my marriage to Margaret all those years ago, I was stifled. I tried so hard to develop feelings for her. Any passion of any kind. But it was a failure. For both of us."

Adelaide thought of Meg. She'd said something similar, and none of it made sense to Adelaide. "How could she kiss you and feel nothing?" she mused, almost more to herself than to him.

He jerked his head up and met her gaze. "I never kissed her."

Adelaide stared at him, a mixture of disbelief and pure pleasure boiling in her chest. "No?"

He shook his head. "I never...*wanted* to. I couldn't picture that future, even in the slightest. So that marriage would have been a horrible trap for both of us. But with you, it is different."

"How so?" she squeaked out, for suddenly his words seemed far less unromantic.

He reached for her hand. "I want you, Adelaide. In a powerful way that I never understood before I kissed you."

She stiffened. "You want Lydia," she corrected.

"No," he said, his jaw tightening. "I'm not talking about Lydia. I told you last night, it's *you*. When I saw Lydia return as we went into the theatre earlier today, I wasn't happy to see her."

"But you told me you were torn between Lydia and me," she whispered. "That was what brought you such trouble, wasn't it?"

He nodded. "But now I know why you created Lydia: to hide. She was a shield against trouble, a barrier between yourself and unhappiness. She was a corner you were forced into. And yes, I cared for her. But what I've come to realize is that everything wonderful about her are all the things that are best about *you*. The real you. Not the spinster wallflower, not the bold actress. *You*. I didn't tell Lydia Ford my secrets. I told *you*. And you are who I want. My Adelaide. The woman who knows me and whose secrets I will protect with my life. The woman who would do the same for me. *That* is who I want. So we will marry, Adelaide."

This was no declaration of love, certainly. And she still ached for that because her own love for this man was so strong and so powerful. But what he offered was still magical. A future with him. And she could see it stretching out in front of her, happy, if she could make it so. If she could accept what he could give and what he couldn't.

In that moment, she hoped she could.

"Are you asking me or are you telling me?" she said with a half-smile for him.

He grinned in response, and that rare and bright expression lit up the whole carriage. "Asking," he said. "Though I'll tell you I won't take no for an answer."

She bent her head. She would have safety. She would have passion, at least until he bored of her. She would have stability because he would ensure it.

And she found herself nodding. "Yes. I will marry you, Graham."

He crossed the carriage in one smooth motion and his mouth was on hers, hard and heavy and filled with passion. She lifted into him, her arms around his neck, her body molded to his as she accepted this offer with everything she was.

He pulled away as the carriage slowed and turned into James and Emma's drive. "I have much to prepare for Melinda and Toby," he said. "And a few things to ready for us, as well. But I'll come back here for supper."

She nodded as the footman opened the door. "I look forward to it."

He kissed her hand and then allowed her to exit. She turned

to watch him go, torn between joy and disappointment. Her whole life she had never expected a love match. And now she had it, at least on her side, and it wasn't enough.

She entered the foyer and was greeted by Grimble. "Is the duchess available?" Adelaide asked as he took her gloves.

"The duke and duchess have taken an afternoon rest," Grimble explained. "The duke was very clear that Her Grace was not to be disturbed until supper."

Adelaide smiled. "After this morning's upset, that is likely best for her and the child."

She looked around. This house was a good home for Emma, but it wasn't Adelaide's home. She thought of her aunt, so devastated by Adelaide's choices. She was the only guardian Adelaide had known since the death of her parents. The only person who had taken care of her. And she *had* taken care of Adelaide. She remembered moments of tenderness between them though they were long ago, when she was still a child.

It was only as she grew older that Opal's anger increased. That her anxiety and accusations were born. But perhaps an engagement to a powerful duke would assuage her. Perhaps there was still some way to maintain a relationship of some kind with the only family she'd ever known.

"Is there something I can do for you, my lady?" Grimble asked.

Adelaide blinked, realizing she had been standing in the foyer beside the poor man, drifting off into fantasy. "I'm sorry, Grimble, I was woolgathering. But do you think you might arrange for a carriage to be brought round for me?"

Grimble nodded. "Of course, Lady Adelaide. What direction should I give to the driver?"

"I'd like to go to Lady Opal's," she explained. "I need to see my aunt."

CHAPTER NINETEEN

Graham sat in the quiet, pretty parlor, looking around as his heart throbbed. He had returned to his home and made his arrangements an hour ago, but a driving voice had been pounding in his head for days. So finally, he had gotten on his horse and come here. To this place he had once vowed to never return.

He moved to the fireplace and looked up. On the wall was mounted a painting of the inhabitants of this place—the Duke and Duchess of Crestwood. Simon and Meg. His best friend and his once fiancée.

Not that long ago, seeing their portrait would have made Graham flinch at Simon's betrayal. Now he saw the picture through very different eyes. He saw the love that was between the pair even in the painted image. She was seated, with Simon standing behind her. His hand rested on her shoulder and her own was lifted to cover his. He glanced down with a small smile, as if he were enraptured by her.

Which of course he was. Always had been, it turned out. And Graham understood that far better now.

The door behind him opened and he turned to find Meg standing there, her eyes wide as she stared at him. She was lovely, she always had been, with chestnut hair and dark eyes and a lively, expressive face. Right now he saw her shock reflected there. Her wariness.

"Graham," she breathed. "My God, when Finley said you'd arrived I thought he had gotten into the mulled wine. But you are here."

Graham took a step toward her. "I am. Does Simon not wish to see me?" he asked as a swell of pain spread through his chest. Perhaps he had waited too long to speak to his friend. Perhaps it was too late.

Meg shook her head. "Oh no, not at all. Simon is out, that is all. He should be back momentarily, and I know he'll want to see you. My God, you're truly here. Please sit. Let me get you tea."

Graham was about to tell her that he didn't want tea, but she was already racing to the sideboard, pouring from the service there and sweetening his drink just as he liked it. Because of course she would remember that detail. This was Meg, after all.

He smiled as he retook his seat and reached for the cup she brought him. "Thank you, Your Grace."

She sat across from him and shook her head. "Oh, please don't do that. It's Meg, it's always been Meg. If you're here I have to hope that it will be Meg again."

He inclined his head in acquiescence. "Very well, Meg. You look well. You look happy."

She hesitated and he could see she questioned how to respond. But at last she nodded. "I *am* happy, Graham. It was difficult at first, of course. Simon and I had our struggles. Even now, there are whispers, which I know you're fully aware of. But I am happy."

"Good," he said softly. "I would hate for all that turmoil and hurt not to have a happy ending for you. You *deserve* happiness and love."

She drew in a sharp breath at that statement. "Thank you, Graham. You deserve the same and more."

He swallowed. He'd come looking for Simon, but now that he was here with the woman he'd once planned to marry, he recognized that she had answers for him, to questions he'd never thought he'd ask.

"When did you know you loved Simon?" he asked.

Meg shifted at the direct question. It clearly made her uncomfortable, like she was betraying him by admitting any part of the truth. But at last she straightened her shoulders and met his eyes. "You want my honesty, yes?"

"I do."

"I was fifteen when I first realized that I loved him," she whispered, her voice thick with emotion, but not regret. "A year before James arranged for my marriage to you. In truth, I had probably loved him since the very first moment I met him."

"*How* did you know?" he asked.

She tilted her head, and he could see her reading him. Meg had always been able to do that with everyone around her. She could see what people were at their core, she could see what they needed. It was her greatest asset and always had been.

"When I pictured my future and could not imagine it without him, I knew." She leaned closer. "And I'm so very sorry I wasn't brave enough to say something to James that very moment. If I had been braver, none of what happened a few months ago would have had to come to pass. And you and Simon both wouldn't have been hurt."

He considered that for a moment. Perhaps months or even weeks ago, that might have been the words he needed to hear. The apology. The admission of guilt. But now…

"I didn't understand what happened at the time, you know. I couldn't understand *how* you two could do what you did. But now, with months between that moment and this one and…and with other things intervening, I think I understand more."

Her expression softened. "Do you? Could you?"

"Yes." He let out a long, heavy sigh. "The heart is not something one can control, is it? We want what we want, there is no arguing or negotiating that. In our case, we were each driven by a need not to hurt anyone else. And instead we were *all* damaged. I don't pretend that you and Simon weren't hurt by what transpired. Nor do I imagine that it could have ended any other way. If you and I had married, it would have been devastating to us all. So I want you to understand something, Meg."

She stared at him, tears glistening in her eyes. "What is that?"

"I'm *glad* it happened." He said the words and he meant them all the way down to his core. All his anger, all his pain, it faded with that acceptance. "I wouldn't change it. We are all where we are meant to be and that couldn't have happened without that night in the cottage between you and Simon."

She drew in a ragged breath. "Does that mean you forgive us? Forgive *him*?"

He nodded, and it was so very true in that moment. A peace filled him, filled every fiber of his being, filled every space in his mind and the universe felt clear. Without the betrayal that had cut him so deeply, he would have married Meg. They would have been miserable. He never would have roamed London aimlessly, he never would have been directed toward Lydia, he never would have found Adelaide.

His life would have been cold and empty and miserable. And now he had a future in front of him. One that was clear and powerful and filled with…love.

He loved Adelaide. He loved her with a power he hadn't known he could possess. And it was terrifying and wonderful and perfect and thrilling all at once. It made him understand everything Simon had done because the idea of someone taking her, someone keeping her from him, made his mind race and his hands shake.

"You *are* here."

Graham got to his feet and turned as Simon entered the room. His friend with the mischievous air to him, with the kindness that permeated everything he did, with the light that had always made the darkness in Graham just a little easier to bear, stared at him. There was pain on his face, but also hope.

Graham said nothing, he just came around the settee, crossed the room to him in three long strides. Simon stiffened, his expression uncertain, but when Graham grabbed his arm and tugged him in for an embrace, Simon's arms folded around him. They stood that way for a moment, then Graham backed away, smiling as Meg stepped up with tears in her eyes.

"I'll leave you two," she said, squeezing Graham's hand before she leaned up to kiss Simon's cheek gently. The couple's eyes met, and a world of love and understanding passed between them. He recognized it now, as he hadn't before because he'd never felt love like that before. Now he did. And he understood everything so much better.

She left, and Simon leaned back to shut the door. "I can't believe you're here," he said. "Sit. She gave you tea, didn't she? Meg and her tea. Would you like something stronger?"

Graham chuckled. "No, I'm fine."

"*I* might need something stronger," Simon muttered as he went to the sideboard and splashed some scotch into a glass. "Finley said you were here and I thought—"

"He was drunk? That was Meg's reaction too."

"Well, we are often of a mind," Simon said with a shrug.

"You are that," Graham said. "I just never understood it. If I had, I would have stepped aside long before that night in the cottage."

Simon flinched as he slowly took the place across from Graham where Meg had last sat. "You were right the last time you talked to me. You were right when you said that I should have done something. It wasn't your responsibility."

"The last time I talked to you, I was very drunk," Graham said with a shake of his head as he thought of a bleary afternoon at White's when he'd tried to force Simon to fight him. "And I was cruel."

"No, you were honest," Simon said. "Which is more than I gave you. But your words that day drove me back to Meg. Drove me to fight for what I wanted, even if I refused to fight you. And you saved us, Graham. I'll never be able to repay that debt. Nor will I be able to apologize enough for my bungling of the matter. I destroyed our friendship, not just that night when Meg and I were trapped together, but for years before that. Because I couldn't look you in the eye and tell you what I wanted."

"Desperation can drive a man to do things he wouldn't normally," Graham said. "And love. I…I understand that more now."

Simon wrinkled his brow. "Are you saying you're in love?"

Graham took a deep breath. "Yes," he admitted, then ran a hand through his hair. "Christ, that's the first time I've said it out loud."

Simon laughed. "Am I correct to guess it is with Lady Adelaide?"

Graham's eyes went wide. "And how do you know that?"

"Meg and Emma are close, remember," Simon said with a shrug. "And Adelaide doesn't think much of Meg. Since *everyone* adores my wife, her reticence made it obvious that Adelaide liked you and was taking your side on the matter."

"Well, her hesitations about Meg will change once she realizes I've forgiven you," Graham said with a smile as he thought of his warrior Adelaide, always on his side. "She's protective of me."

"She is." Simon leaned forward. "Do you truly forgive me?"

Graham nodded. "Yes."

"And are you planning on marrying this woman who has tempted you to love?" Simon pressed, his tone much lighter now. It was like old times, in fact. Old times when Simon had been the one he could say certain things to. Things that needed gentleness or finesse or lightness.

"I am," Graham said slowly. "We made the agreement earlier today, though I haven't yet told her my feelings."

Simon wrinkled his brow. "No? Why?"

"We've been a bit forced into it," Graham said with a shake of his head. "That seems to go around in our group, doesn't it?"

"We've all been dragged into our futures thus far, yes," Simon conceded. "But it's been a very worthwhile endeavor for James and for me. If you love her, you'll find a way to make it work. And I tell you, loving them is well worth any price you'd pay."

Graham nodded. "Yes, I can see that now. I can understand it for the first time. Truly, aside from my lack of honesty about my heart, there is only one mar on our future together."

Simon cocked his head. "What is that?"

"Her aunt," Graham mused, thinking of the rage on Lady Opal's face when she had lunged at Adelaide. Thinking of Adelaide's confession that the woman had been physically abusive a handful of times in the past. "The woman is jealously protective of her charge's virtue. And she is violently angry at Adelaide's actions."

"But if your intentions are true, isn't it possible you could soften her to you and to Adelaide?" Simon suggested. "Talk to her?"

Graham paused. It had been impossible for him to see past the anger Lady Opal had expressed. It triggered a response in him that was almost out of his control. But he knew that Adelaide still thought of her aunt as her only family. Her defense of the woman proved that. And Simon could be correct that a conversation might soften the response.

And if not, Graham could firmly tell the woman that if she ever laid a hand on Adelaide again, she would be very sorry indeed.

He glanced at Simon. The peacemaker of their group, he had managed many a rough encounter. "I don't suppose you'd want to accompany me on this mission?"

Simon's lips parted. "You would want my help?"

Graham nodded. "You don't know how many times I wanted to talk to you in the past few months. But now more than ever I need your counsel."

Simon reached out and squeezed Graham's forearm. "Of course. After all, how could this woman even think to turn down two powerful dukes? One of whom actually has charm."

Graham tilted his head back and laughed, and it was like that motion bled away all the remaining vestiges of his pain and his betrayal. It reminded him of how much he loved his friend.

His brother.

"Good," he said, rising to his feet. "Then let's go now."

"Now?" Simon repeated with a laugh. "You really do love this girl."

"I do," Graham said, and each time he said it, the emotion grew stronger in his chest. "So help me win her, will you?"

Adelaide had been waiting long enough for her aunt in the parlor that she was beginning to become nervous. Especially since the home had become increasingly quiet over the past half hour. The sounds of servants bustling had faded and no one had come to check on her or see if she required refreshments.

She could only assume that was on her aunt's order. Which meant Opal was still angry with her.

She drew in a deep breath at the thought. What would she do if her aunt raged at her? If she refused to forgive or to accept the future that Adelaide would now pursue?

"I'll leave," she said with a sigh as she scrubbed a hand over her face. "I'll leave and go to Graham. I'll accept that my future is where I belong."

She said the words and smiled, for in that moment the future felt very bright, indeed.

The door behind her opened, and she turned to face Opal. Her aunt was wearing the same gown she had had on when she'd come to call at James and Emma's home earlier in the day. Only now there were smudges on it, like she had been doing some kind of work in the outfit.

Adelaide frowned. "Good afternoon, Aunt Opal."

She tensed as she waited for her guardian to respond. To get angry. To lash out. Instead, her aunt merely inclined her head. "Hello, Adelaide. I'm so sorry I didn't come sooner. I wasn't expecting you after that terrible scene at the Duke and Duchess of Abernathe's."

Adelaide drew in a short breath at the softness of her aunt's tone. She actually did look and sound regretful. That gave Adelaide hope. "Yes. It *was* terrible. I'm so sorry you were upset that I went to Emma's home. You must know I never intended to stay away forever. This is the only home I've known for most of my life."

Opal's lip twitched and she held Adelaide's stare for what felt like forever before she said, "Why don't you come up to your room with me?"

Adelaide wrinkled her brow at the odd request. "Why?"

"I want to show you something," Opal insisted, motioning for Adelaide to lead the way. "And talk to you, calmly this time, rationally, about what we must do for the future."

Adelaide pressed her lips together. She was often ill at ease with Opal, especially in the past few years, but right now she wondered at the cause for the stirring in her stomach. Opal was being sensible, after all, even kind.

Adelaide nodded at last. "Very well. Let's go to my chamber."

She walked up the stairs with Opal beside her, passing by portraits of family members on the wall. Opal hesitated beside the one of Adelaide's parents. "My dear brother," she said with a sigh. "And his lovely wife. They cared for me so deeply. They tried to save me."

Adelaide wrinkled her brow. In the entire decade and a half that she had lived under her aunt's roof, she could count on one hand the times Opal had spoken of Adelaide's parents. When she had, it wasn't with the wistfulness her tone presented now.

"Save you?" she repeated. "That's an odd turn of phrase. How did they do that?"

Opal ignored her and started up the stairs again. "What happened today is very likely something we can't cover up, Adelaide. Not like the last time."

Adelaide flinched at the comparison of Graham to a man who had left her after one unpleasant night together. "No, you are probably right," she said softly. "But the circumstances are very different. You see..." She took a deep breath, uncertain how her aunt would respond to her next words. "Graham is going to marry me," she pushed out at last.

They had reached the top of the stairs then, and her aunt froze and turned on her, her eyes wide. "Is that what he's said?"

"Yes. He asked me after you left, and I agreed. So you see, it isn't as bad as you thought it was in the parlor this morning. This time I have found myself with a very decent man. One who will not abandon me."

Her aunt nodded slowly and continued into the bedchamber. Adelaide looked around. It was a simple room, yes. Her aunt had never encouraged her to decorate it overly much. But it had been hers for a long time, and she didn't hate the place.

Opal paced to the window and looked down over the garden in the back of the house. "When you marry, he will want heirs. Spares."

Adelaide found herself smiling at the thought of starting a family with Graham. Of him becoming the father he had never had. Of looking into her children's eyes and seeing all the echoes of the man she loved. All the best of both of them.

"Yes," she said. "Yes, I'm certain we will. He has obligations, of course. And I would want to be a mother."

Opal pursed her lips. "Then it will not stop."

Adelaide wrinkled her brow in confusion. "Will not stop?" she repeated. "Aunt Opal, I came back here today to tell you of my impending marriage, but also to ask if you will support it. You are my only living family, after all. I know we've had our differences and that I've let you down with my behavior, but I *do* want your blessing."

Opal moved toward her a step. "Your only family," she repeated with a shake of her head. "My, how right you are. More right than you even know."

The hairs on Adelaide's neck began to prickle as she stared at her calm aunt. Far too calm the morning's outburst. Suddenly her room didn't feel as safe as it once had, and she began to question if coming here was so very wise.

"I don't understand what you mean," she whispered, looking toward the door.

Opal sighed. "I know. And I thought I might not ever have to tell you. But it seems I must. To end this, I must have it all out."

"What all out?"

Opal motioned toward the settee. "Sit."

It was an order, not a request, and her aunt was blocking her way to the exit. Adelaide had no choice, it seemed, but to obey. She sank into the settee and folded her suddenly trembling hands in her lap.

"I was like you," Opal began. "When I was young. Foolish and headstrong. And I met a young man and I thought he was a knight in shining armor. That he would sweep me away."

Adelaide's lips parted in surprise. "I've seen your portraits from when you were young. You were so beautiful. I'm not surprised that you had suitors, but we've never spoken of them."

"This man was not a suitor," her aunt spat, a flash of anger to her tone and her eyes. "He was a thief in the night, come to seduce an innocent girl and steal what she should never have given."

Adelaide straightened. "Are you speaking of the young man who took my virtue?" she asked, utterly confused.

"No, the one who took mine," Opal replied. Her lips began to tremble. "I did not give, but he took."

Adelaide shut her eyes, understanding at last. She thought of Melinda, her battered face, her haunted eyes. She thought of a dozen other women she knew who had been subject to such abuse. She thought of Sir Archibald's fat hands on her, of that moment when she'd known her fate before Graham burst through the door like some hero in a story to save her.

"I'm so very sorry, Aunt Opal," she breathed. "I had no idea you suffered such a thing."

Opal's gaze was far away, years away. "Oh yes, I suffered. My father cut me off, as I presented no more hope for a good match. And when I began to swell with that bastard's child, I was forced to go into seclusion in my brother's home."

Adelaide stared. This was not a story she knew. Not a story anyone had told her. "You had a child?"

Opal jerked out one nod. "I did. No one knew. My brother and his wife hid what I'd done from the world. And when the baby came...they *pretended*."

Her aunt's words sank in, and Adelaide rose from the couch, her hands shaking as all the blood rushed from her face and made her dizzy with horror and understanding. "Pretended? Are you saying...are you saying that your brother and his wife took in the child? Pretended the baby was their own?"

"I didn't want you," Opal hissed, rising as well and glaring at Adelaide. "I looked at you and I saw that horrible night. A reminder of *him*."

Adelaide lifted a hand to her lips. "You are lying," she said. "You are deranged. They were my parents. No one ever hinted otherwise. I was theirs."

Opal shook her head. "No, you were *mine*. You stole my future and my hopes, and I loved you and hated you so very much."

Adelaide was shaking so hard, she was hardly able to stay upright. She stared at her aunt. Oh, she'd always seen the similarities between them. The faint reminder that her aunt's hair had been blonde before she went gray. The hands that were the same. The lips.

But she'd always chalked those things up being family. She'd never thought, not once, not ever, that the woman who raised her, who held her at arm's length, who gave her only the bare minimum of support, was her mother.

"If that is true, why did you take me when they died?" she whispered, her voice cracking on every word, because the truth of what was being said was starting to sink into her body, her skin, her soul.

It was tearing her apart piece by piece.

"Because no one else wanted you. And I knew that their deaths were my penance being forced back on me. So I took you.

And I prayed you wouldn't be like him."

"Him?" Adelaide's stomach turned as she comprehended what Opal meant. "How can you compare me to a man who forced himself on you?"

"You are a wanton, Adelaide!" her aunt roared. "You were for that boy, that boy who came mooning about. I saw what you were then. I thought I could stop it by stopping him."

"Stopping him," Adelaide repeated, backing up a step. "What does that mean? How did you stop him? He left."

Her aunt shook her head slowly. "I let you believe that, hoping that you would recognize your true nature and work to better yourself. To rise above your natural tendencies."

"What did you do?" Adelaide asked.

"I killed him," Opal said. "I killed him."

Adelaide staggered backward, as far as she could from her aunt. Until her back hit the window, until there was nowhere else to run. No way to hide from the horror that her aunt spewed at her.

"No," she said. "No, that isn't possible."

"It very much is." Her aunt was nodding and nodding, like her head was on a hinge. "You pay a man enough and he'll help you get rid of a body and make it look like he left London of his own volition. So I did."

Adelaide covered her mouth with both hands, praying she wouldn't cast up her accounts then and there. She thought of that man, Charlie, who she had taught herself to hate. Taught herself to forget because she'd believed he'd used and discarded her.

Now she knew better.

"Poor Charlie," she sobbed. "Oh God, Aunt Opal, how could you?"

"So you would stop!" her aunt burst out. "I had to make you stop. And you did, for a long time. You wore the clothing to cover your shame, you stood along the wall as you should. You hid away as was your destiny. But then *he* appeared."

"Graham," Adelaide whispered, and came forward a long step. "You will not hurt him, Opal. I'll not let you. You will not hurt a hair on his head."

"No," her aunt agreed, walking across the room. She picked up a small statue that she'd given Adelaide years ago. A figure of Persephone, forever torn between two worlds. Forever punished by both her lover and her mother.

Now Adelaide stared at it, and everything made such perfect sense.

"I'm not going to hurt him," her aunt continued as she moved forward. "Because I realize that it is *you* who must be silenced. Stopped. Or else you will make more spawn like you who will only do worse. We are damaged women, Adelaide. And the only way to stop it is to die."

She swung the statue, and Adelaide lifted her hands with a scream. But she couldn't block the heavy statue as it hit her in the side of the head. She slid down the wall staring up at her aunt, her mother. The world was spinning, going black. She had to fight it, had to stop it, but it was too powerful. Too strong.

And she slipped into unconsciousness with one thought in her mind.

Graham.

CHAPTER TWENTY

Graham and Simon were laughing as they turned their mounts into the drive of Lady Opal's small but fine London home. Graham couldn't remember the last time he'd felt so light. He loved Adelaide, he had reunited with Simon and if all went well, he could even find a way to manage Opal so that Adelaide could still have some family. But as they approached the house, his smile fell.

"That's James's carriage," he said, pointing at the stable, where a carriage was parked. There were no other servants around it, but he recognized the crest and his friend's driver leaning against the wheel as he smoked.

Simon looked at him. "Would James have a reason to come here? Perhaps to talk to Lady Opal as we've planned?"

Graham's heart had begun to pound as the two men swung down on the drive. "No," he said softly. "I don't think it's James who had the carriage take him here. I think it's Adelaide."

Simon looked up at the house. "By now we should have had footmen coming down, the butler opening the door. It's awfully quiet."

"Too quiet," Graham agreed. "Damn it, I hope she didn't come here by herself. Her aunt is…troubled."

"Is she capable of hurting Adelaide?" Simon asked.

Graham nodded and his chest hurt. "Yes."

"Come on," Simon insisted, taking the stairs up to the door

two at a time. "No time to waste."

Graham passed him at full speed and didn't stop to knock on the door. He pushed at it and growled as he found it locked. He leaned back and kicked, once, twice, and the lock gave way, throwing the door inward into an eerily quiet foyer that was thick with smoke.

"Christ!" Simon said, waving his hand. "The house is on fire! I'll have James's man call for the brigade, then I'll come in to help you search."

But Graham didn't answer. He leapt into the hazy foyer, ducking low to try to get beneath the worst of the cloying, choking smoke.

"Adelaide!" he called out, panic gripping him. She was here. He knew it, he sensed it down to his bones. She was here and this fire was no accident, not if the lack of servants was any indication.

"Adelaide!" he screamed, choking as the smoke filled his lungs. He rushed up the stairs, though he had no idea if she was up or down. But the smoke was filling the space, and he knew it would rise before it fully took over the lower levels. His best bet was to start at the top and hope.

He came around the corner into the hallway at the top of the stairs and skidded to a halt. A fire had been set right in front of a door, and it licked up the walls and across the barrier.

Adelaide's room. He could have bet on it. He rushed forward, stomping at the growing flames as he tried to reach the door.

"Adelaide!" he screamed at the top of his lungs.

For a moment there was silence, and then a weak voice on the other side of the door. "Graham! Graham, please."

He gave no more thought to the flames, to the danger. Adelaide was in that room and he rushed forward, ignoring the searing pain as the fire licked at his clothing and his skin. He kicked this door as he'd kicked the other, and it flew open.

What he saw inside nearly stopped his heart. Flames crawled along the walls, and in the middle of the room, tied to a chair, was Adelaide. Her blonde hair was down around her face, there was a huge cut across her temple that left trails of blood through the soot from the fire. She lifted her head, her gaze bleary from smoke and her injury.

"Help me," she whispered, her voice almost not carrying in the hot room.

He leapt to her, untying her from the chair before he gathered her up against his chest and ran through the room, where the beams above creaked under the weight of their disintegrating wood, through the flaming door that was hot as hell. He ducked low, racing down the stairs and out the front door where he took in a gulp of air.

Simon was already outside helping neighboring servants as they fought the flames with a bucket brigade. Graham rushed Adelaide away from the house and set her down on the grass beyond the drive gingerly.

"She's not breathing!" he screamed as the truth of it became clear. "Help me!"

Simon dropped down next to him, staring at the motionless body of the love of Graham's life. He looked as helpless as Graham felt. "Lucas wrote to me once," Simon said, his gaze lighting up. "About sharing breath with an injured person. Put your mouth on hers and breathe into her."

Graham lifted her, positioning his mouth over hers as he gently blew air past her lips. Once, twice, but she didn't stir. Three times as tears stung his eyes, dripped down his cheeks.

"Please," he begged before he gave her one last long gust.

To his pure relief, she coughed, turning her head as she gasped and dragged in great gulps of clean air. He collapsed down next to her, pulling her against him, pressing kisses to her bloody and grimy face as the fire burned behind them and destroyed everything but the most important thing in the world.

Adelaide turned her head, and an explosion of pain worked through her entire skull. She moaned against it, lifting a hand to touch her face. She found it tender and carefully opened her eyes.

She was lying in a bed, propped up on the pillows, and next to her Graham lay on his side, facing her. He was asleep. His cheeks were streaked with soot and his hand rested on her stomach beneath the blankets.

Memories returned, dark and horrible. Of her aunt's terrible confessions. Of the pain as she was struck. Of waking to the room in flame. She couldn't hold back a sob as all those things mobbed her.

Graham opened his eyes at the sound and reached for her, pulling her tight against his chest as he pressed a kiss to her uninjured temple. "I know," he whispered. "It's all right. I'm here."

She cried into his shoulder for a while, and he never spoke. He never demanded. He never did anything but gently rock her, offering her comfort where there was none. It was only when he lifted a hand to touch her face that she noticed the bandages on his arms, his hands.

She gasped out a sound of horror and tried to sit up, but was met with another explosion of pain through her skull.

"It's all right," he soothed. "The burns aren't very bad. And you are well. You're safe. I would have lit myself entirely on fire without hesitation to ensure that."

She felt hot tears running down her cheeks and buried her face back into his shoulder. She smelled smoke on his clothing and it jerked her back, once again, to the horrible, bleary moments in the house when she'd known that she would die.

And why.

"Tell me what happened," he whispered, his lips soft against her ear.

She let out a shuddering sigh and told him everything. He said nothing, just allowed her to pause when she needed to catch her breath, let her weep when the tears came. When it was all over, he just held her, trembling just as she did.

"Do you think it's true?" Adelaide asked, sinking back against the pillows with a shuddering sigh.

He rolled to his side and traced her cheek with his fingertip. "I don't know. There are a lot of details to the story for it to be a lie. And it would explain her strong reactions to me, to Charlie, to you."

She stared up at the ceiling. "I *know* it's true."

He was quiet a long time and she appreciated his silence. He was allowing her to process what she'd been through. Allowing her to feel whatever came into her heart rather than trying to push it away and offer false comfort before she was ready.

But at last her mind stilled a little. She glanced at him. "Why were you there?"

He smiled, just a tiny lift of his lips. "I came with Simon, to try to make your aunt see reason."

"With Simon?" she repeated. "Does that mean—"

He nodded, and in that moment she saw what a weight had been lifted from his shoulders. "I went to see him. I talked to Meg and to him for a long time. And though there is likely still time left for all of us to fully heal, we're on the road to it. He gave me the tools to save your life. Thank God he was there." She touched his sooty face and he smiled again. "I apologize for the mess. They couldn't make me leave your side."

"I don't care about the ash. I'm so glad you're here with me. But what about my aunt's servants?"

He sighed and her heart lurched. "She had sent them all away the moment you returned. Your butler, Finley, thought it odd and had rushed to find someone to help. We were lucky that the Home Office was already on its way and the fire brigade soon followed. They couldn't save your aunt's home, but they kept the blaze from spreading to the surrounding buildings."

"Thank God for that," Adelaide said with a shake of her head. "My aunt could have taken out the entire neighborhood. Half the city. For what? To stop me from being...*me*?" She hesitated and met his eyes. "What of her?"

He frowned deeply. "I'm so sorry, Adelaide, but…but they found her in the parlor. She didn't survive."

She shut her eyes, tears stinging yet again. "We had such a complicated relationship. Indifference, cruelty, occasional bursts of loving affection when I was a little girl…but she was all I had left in this world. I suppose I should take some solace that she's at peace now. Whatever troubles plagued her, whatever truth was within her lies and delusions, she's not in pain anymore."

"You are better than I am," Graham said. "I could offer her no such peace after what she did to you."

"But I'm here. And you're here. And in the end, she only harmed herself in any way that will stick." She traced his lips gently, loving how close he was. Loving him with all her heart. And since she had almost lost him, she knew what she had to do. "I must tell you something."

He nodded slowly. "Anything, you should know that by now."

She cleared her throat and felt heat in her cheeks. This moment was so abjectly terrifying. But she needed to take it. Right now she knew better than most that there might not be another. Life could be taken so unexpectedly. She didn't want regrets, not ever again.

"I have fallen in love with you, Graham," she said. She held up a hand to keep him from speaking. "I don't expect you to feel the same. I don't want you to say anything you don't mean—we both know how damaging that can be. But there was a moment today when I realized I would not live. And the idea that I would die without telling you my heart was as painful as anything else I endured. I vowed that if I survived, I wouldn't be afraid of your rejection. That I'd tell you the truth."

"Are you finished?" he asked.

She shifted. "I-I suppose so, yes."

"I almost lost you, as well," he said. "But that didn't inspire me to tell you I loved you."

Her heart sank. She hadn't expected him to be so direct about it. "I understand."

He shook his head. "No, you don't. I intended to tell you I loved you the very next time I saw you, Adelaide, long before I saw the fire and realized you were trapped. I intended to tell you, just as I'm telling you now, that you possess my heart in every way."

Her lips parted and disbelief shook her. "No," she said, and moved as much as she could.

He caught her arm gently. "Don't you dare run from me now. Neither of us has felt much love in our lives. Don't think for a moment that this feeling doesn't terrify me as much as it terrifies you. Or that I don't fear that I'll somehow destroy whatever we could possibly build. I *do* fear that. But I fear walking away from you more. I love you, Adelaide. You and only you. And the future can be far better than the past. That is what you've shown me from the first moment I saw you walk out on stage weeks ago."

She felt the heat of her tears on her cheeks once more, but this time they weren't tears of pain or devastation. They were tears of joy. Tears of acceptance that everything he said was real and true and right. That they would love each other and teach each other how to love. That they would have the rest of their lives to explore what it was to be fully accepted and fully adored.

Because she did adore him. And looking into his bright eyes, she could see all her feelings were returned.

She didn't speak. She leaned up, drawing him down into her, lifting her mouth to his and kissing him with all her passion and her love, and the hopes and dreams she had long ago put away. With him, she had more than ever.

When he pulled away, he grinned, and it brightened the very room with happiness and light and hope. "Oh, there is one more thing. My carriage did retrieve Melinda and Toby, and they are on the way to my estate without incident. I thought that would please you."

She struggled to sit up, her head spinning. Once that feeling had passed, she looked at him evenly. "Actually, I think there is a way for us to save them without hideouts and solicitors and every other wonderful thing you've planned in that brilliant mind of yours."

His brow wrinkled. "Thwarting my plans again, are you? Tell me."

She drew in a long breath. "My assumption is that when I marry you, Lydia Ford will be no more."

"I-I hadn't considered that. Would you be unhappy turning away from the stage?"

She blinked at the question. At the idea that he would have no issue with her continuing. And all her love swelled higher.

"You know I performed as a way to escape my real life, but I never thought it could truly last," she reminded him. "Even if it could, I don't want to escape you. Ever. So my thought is that Lydia must play one grand final part."

He nodded. "I'm listening."

"Everyone saw what happened between Sir Archibald and you the night he attacked me. But they also know that *Lydia* suffered at his hands. Does it not follow that she could have lured him back to the theatre and exacted her revenge?"

He leaned back and considered it a moment, then he grinned. "That is...*brilliant*, actually."

"Thank you." She said with her own smile. "So Lydia will write a letter explaining what she did and then expressing how the guilt wracks her and she cannot go on. She will drown in the Thames as penance for her crime."

"Very dramatic," he said, voice solemn though his eyes were bright with teasing. "But what about Melinda and Toby? Your friend adores you, she would be brokenhearted."

She worried her lip. "Yes, there is that. I would hate to have her suffer thinking I was dead. But what if we...told them the truth?"

"Could you trust them?" he asked.

She nodded without hesitation. "Yes."

"Well, I need a new manager of the very estate I've sent

them to," he said. "I could offer Toby a job if he'd like it. He has experience in the theatre. And then you'll still get to see Melinda."

She couldn't help but grin with enthusiasm and then winced as the pain in her head returned. He frowned and wrapped his arms around her, lowering her back on the pillows as he looked over her face with concern.

"I assume Emma has been waiting to see me," she said. "Worried sick. I have so much to tell her."

"You do," he said with a soft smile. "But it can wait. Have I mentioned in the past five minutes that I love you, Adelaide?"

She laughed despite all the pain that had been caused in the last forty-eight hours. Pain that she knew would fade with time and with the happiness she would find for the rest of her life with this glorious man.

"It's been six or seven," she said.

"Then I would be remiss if I didn't say that I do love you, Adelaide."

She tugged him down to kiss her once more. And before their lips met, she whispered, "I love you, Graham. With all my heart."

EPILOGUE

Graham entered Emma and James's breakfast room to find Adelaide seated with a paper spread out before her. She smiled up at him and his world seemed to brighten in that instant.

He had hardly left her side since the fire a week before. He hadn't wanted to after nearly losing her. Somehow he had even convinced Emma to allow him to stay in Adelaide's chamber each night. At first he'd just held her, but in the last two nights, as her injuries had healed, she had opened herself to him again and all his passion returned. It seemed it would never fade, and he was glad of it. Making her sigh with pleasure was one of the best experiences of his life.

"It's in this morning's paper," she said, pointing to the words slashed across the Society pages and drawing his attention back to the moment at hand.

"'London's Most Infamous Actress Admits to Murder'," he read out loud. "Suicide suspected, body not yet found."

She nodded, though she twisted her mouth slightly. "I never thought I was London's most *infamous* actress."

He laughed at her unexpected pouting. "You are now. They will be talking about you for years to come."

"Probably right to my face, without even knowing that I'm the one they're speaking of," she grumbled.

He leaned forward and kissed her, silencing her grousing in the most happy of ways. "That's what you want, my dear, never forget it."

She shrugged. "I suppose you are correct."

"Are you and Emma and Meg going out today?" he asked.

Her smile widened. "Yes. My first time out since the fire. I must say, I do like Meg. She's very kind."

He nodded, and there was no hesitation as he said, "She is. She always has been."

"You know, you really do seem so much more at ease now that you've ended your feud with Simon," she said.

He cocked his head. "Is that what you think? That my reunion with Simon is the cause of my lightness?"

"It is, isn't it?"

He caught both her hands in his and tugged until she staggered from her chair and into his lap. "I will admit that my reunion with my friends takes a weight from my shoulders that was terribly heavy. But if I am happy, if I am light, if I am at peace with the future…that, my dear, is all because of *you*."

She leaned down, brushing her lips against his. When she parted from him, she said, "I heard you and James talking about the wedding last night when we rejoined you two after your port. You know, now that my aunt is gone, there is no need to rush."

He lifted both brows. "I object to that statement. There is most definitely a need to rush. I adore you and I want to call you my wife as soon as possible."

She blushed. "When you say that it still doesn't feel real to me sometimes."

He drew his fingers into her hair, gently cupping her scalp. Slowly, he guided her lips back to his, and just before he claimed her mouth once more, he said, "Well, I must endeavor to make it feel very real…right now."

And he kissed her, making everything right in his world once more. All because of her.

Charlotte tossed her maid an apologetic look as the carriage jerked on the slippery, sleety road. Sylvie looked terrified and Charlotte couldn't blame her. It was the very worst of conditions. Cold permeated the carriage and the blankets tucked around them and rain slicked down the windows, hardening to ice within moments so that one couldn't rightly see outside.

Not that Charlotte needed to see the house to know it. When Ewan had inherited three years ago, his aunt had insisted on a ball to celebrate. She had come with Nathan and slipped away to memorize every line and cranny of Ewan's home.

She shook her head and reached out to touch Sylvie's hand. "We're almost there now, dear."

The girl's teeth chattered as she said, "Y-Yes, my lady."

And as if she had timed it out, the carriage came to a stop at that very moment and it rocked as their driver and footman began to climb down. Charlotte heard voices, both those of her servants and of others rushing to help. She released her maid's hand and straightened up, her heart racing as those outside struggled with the door. Finally it burst open and a swirl of cold air greeted her. She turned her face away from it and when she looked back there was Hargrove Castle, Ewan's estate, looming behind her driver.

"Be careful, my lady, the stairs are rightly slick," Watson said as he offered her not one but two arms to support herself.

She gingerly stepped down onto the drive and stretched her back, ignoring the icy rain that slashed across her face and dampened her hair. "Home," she whispered.

"I beg your pardon, my lady?" Watson said over his

shoulder as he helped Sylvie down the same way.

"Nothing, Watson. Do get as much help as you can with unloading. There is no rush, just be careful. I want no one hurt so that I can have extra gowns, do you understand?"

He faced her with a bow. "Of course, my lady. Would you like Reggie's help up the stairs to the house?"

She glanced at the stone steps. "No, they look as though Smith has had them salted, smart man. I should be fine. And Sylvie, go in and warm up! There is truly no rush for my things."

Her maid nodded and followed another servant around to the back entrance to the house as half a dozen men came rushing to help unload the trunks and portmanteaus.

The door opened as she reached the top and she raced inside the warm foyer. Smith was waiting for her and he shut out the cold and left her to drip onto his lovely, clean floor.

"Oh Smith, we have survived," she said, laughing as she reached up to touch her wet hair. She likely looked like a drowned rat standing before him, but he smiled at her in welcoming nonetheless.

"My lady, how wonderful to see you," he said, "May I take your coat and gloves? I do not see a hat?"

"I took it off in the carriage and like a ninny forgot all about it when I got out," she explained. "I must have been too excited to be here."

"And we are thrilled to have you, my lady. The roads are treacherous, we were worried."

She nodded. "They were indeed. We slid the entire last quarter mile. I know my servants have earned a good warm meal and a rest after that."

"We're ready for them," Smith assured her. "And their dinner shall be warming, indeed."

He was likely going to ask her more. Ask her about tea or showing her to her room. But before he could, Ewan stepped into the foyer. Well, into it was going too far. He stepped up to the edge of the foyer and stopped, just staring at her from across the room.

And she stared back. She couldn't help it. Every time she

saw Ewan, he was more beautiful than the last time. He was tall, well over six feet, with broad shoulders and trim hips. He had blonde hair but it was too long and he never wore it in a queue so it fell around his face. A face he tried to cover with a beard, but that never worked. There was no covering up perfection.

His brown gaze never moved from her and she swallowed hard as her body reacted to his presence and his stare and…just him. Always him. Only him. He was her everything and he had been for her entire life.

She shivered and shook off her thoughts. "You are lurking, dear Ewan," she said, forcing herself to be light and airy so that he wouldn't see that he made her shake far more than any stormy winter's day could.

He smiled. A small smile but it brightened his face and made him even more handsome than before. It was quite unfair, really.

Smith nodded to her. "Excuse me, my lady, I will oversee the unloading."

He left the foyer and then they were alone. She swallowed hard as Ewan stepped closer, closer until he was right in front of her, towering over her, staring down at her and smelling of warmth and man and clean skin.

"You're soaked," he signed in the old language they had concocted over the years. It had been meant to make it easier for him to communicate with his friends, but it had become so complicated that no one else seemed to be able to learn it.

And so, as Meg had suggested a week ago, it was theirs.

She shifted at the words he'd used. If only he knew. She was soaked, but not just from the storm. She wanted him. And his double entendre, even if it was unintended, did not help matters.

"I am," she whispered, her voice husky in the quiet room.

There was a flicker over his face and then it was gone. He signed, "Smith will see to everything. Let me show you up to your room so you can get warm."

She nodded. "That would be wonderful, thank you Ewan."

They stood for a breath and then he slowly extended his

elbow. She reached for him, everything coming in half-time and when she touched him, her body jolted with electric awareness. It was always like this with him.

He guided her through the foyer and up the stairs as she said meaningless words about the roads and the weather and the bridge that one had to cross to get to his estate.

He didn't sign anything in response, but nodded in the appropriate places of her prattling. Finally they reached a door and he released her to open it. She stepped inside and took a breath. It was the same room where she had stayed on her last visit. A beautiful room that overlooked the garden and further off, the sea. Or it would once the storm stopped obliterating all evidence of the ocean in the distance.

When she had visited before the room had been plain, but now it was bright and happy. The walls were a soft pink color, there were somehow flowers on the table, despite the time of year. Everything was perfect.

And once again she got that sense that she was home.

She pushed it aside and turned toward him. "Lovely, Ewan. So beautiful."

He held her stare for a beat too long and then nodded.

"When do you expect the others?" she asked, running a finger along the edge of a pitcher that had been set on the table beside the window. "I hope soon, for the roads are so very treacherous, I worry about Baldwin and mother and Matthew and your aunt."

There was another flicker across his face and then he signed, "I'm afraid they may not make it, Charlotte. You see, my servants closed the bridge behind you after you crossed. It is too treacherous for anyone to try to make it over now. The rest will be stopped at the inn in Donburrow and accommodated there until it is safe to travel again."

"Oh," she said, blinking as shock settled over her at this unexpected news. "I see. Well, of course, the river was so high under the bridge, it could be overrun."

He nodded. "It was last year."

She continued, "And all that ice. So tomorrow then?"

He swallowed and she watched the action with fascination. Every move he made was so very…elegant. And yet still strong and masculine. Even a swallow obsessed her beyond reason or decorum.

"The rain is expected for a day or two more," he signed. "It could take even more than that for the water to recede enough to pass the bridge. It might be up to a week before they can pass."

Her mouth dropped open. What he was saying was sinking in and her reaction was so complicated that she could hardly parse terror from joy from excitement. "Oh. Oh, I see. Are you saying you and I will be…alone…for a week?"

He nodded and to her surprise his gaze slowly flitted over her from the top of her head to the hem of her skirt. In that one slow stare, she saw what she could not deny. Desire. Ewan *did* desire her, it seemed there was no seduction required to inspire that in him.

And suddenly this trip, this storm, everything that was happening seemed like…*providence.*

"Well you and I have always been good company to each other," she said, trying to maintain some normalcy so she wouldn't scare him off when she felt so very close to having what she wanted. "I don't mind if you don't."

"I don't mind," he signed, quickly, without hesitation.

She nodded. "Very well. Then I'll ready myself and see you at supper?"

"Seven o'clock," he signed.

"Seven," she repeated, proud that she could keep the tremble from her voice.

"I'll have your maid sent up," he signed. Then he gave her a little wave and left, closing the door behind himself.

When he was gone, she sagged against the table. Since her shocking talk with Meg last week she had been going back and forth about what to do when it came to Ewan. Take the chance on seduction or leave things be and never risk another rejection?

She hadn't been able to make up her spinning mind on the subject, but now the universe seemed to have intervened on her behalf. Like some greater force *wanted* her to pursue this man.

To take the chance that had always seemed so impossible.

And in truth, she wanted that too. More than anything. More than breath. If this were to be her opportunity, she had to take it and hope that the results would be everything she'd ever hoped for or dreamed about.

Other Books by Jess Michaels

THE 1797 CLUB

For information about the upcoming series, go to
www.1797club.com to join the club!

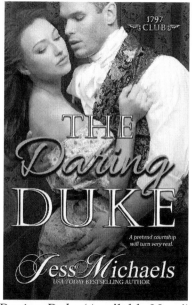

The Daring Duke (Available Now!)
The Broken Duke (Coming September 2017)
The Silent Duke (Coming November 2017)
The Duke of Nothing (Coming January 2018)
The Undercover Duke (Coming March 2018)
The Duke of Hearts (Coming May 2018)
The Duke Who Lied (Coming August 2018)
The Duke of Desire (Coming October 2018)
The Last Duke (Coming November 2018)

SEASONS

An Affair in Winter (Book 1)
A Spring Deception (Book 2)
One Summer of Surrender (Book 3)
Adored in Autumn (Book 4)

THE WICKED WOODLEYS

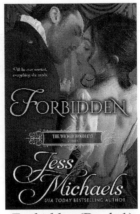

Forbidden (Book 1)
Deceived (Book 2)
Tempted (Book 3)
Ruined (Book 4)
Seduced (Book 5)

THE NOTORIOUS FLYNNS
The Other Duke (Book 1)
The Scoundrel's Lover (Book 2)
The Widow Wager (Book 3)
No Gentleman for Georgina (Book 4)
A Marquis for Mary (Book 5)

THE LADIES BOOK OF PLEASURES
A Matter of Sin
A Moment of Passion
A Measure of Deceit

THE PLEASURE WARS SERIES
Taken By the Duke
Pleasuring The Lady
Beauty and the Earl
Beautiful Distraction

About the Author

Jess Michaels writes erotic historical romance from her home in Tucson, AZ with her husband and one adorable kitty cat. She has written over 50 books, enjoys long walks in the desert and once wrestled a bear over a piece of pie. One of these things is a lie.

Jess loves to hear from fans! So please feel free to contact her in any of the following ways (or carrier pigeon):

www.AuthorJessMichaels.com

Email: Jess@AuthorJessMichaels.com
Twitter www.twitter.com/JessMichaelsbks
Facebook: www.facebook.com/JessMichaelsBks

Jess Michaels raffles a gift certificate EVERY month to members of her newsletter, so sign up on her website: http://www.authorjessmichaels.com/

Made in the USA
Middletown, DE
26 March 2019